CALVARY

FRANK MATHIS

authorHOUSE®

AuthorHouse™
1663 Liberty Drive
Bloomington, IN 47403
www.authorhouse.com
Phone: 1-800-839-8640

Published by AuthorHouse   04/10/2012

ISBN: 978-1-4685-8521-6 (sc)
ISBN: 978-1-4685-8681-7 (e)

Library of Congress Control Number: 2012906536

Calvary

By invitation from his mother's big brother in Montana. Johnathan Olson, went to spend summer at his Uncle's ranch. Everything went well for awhile, till some strange things began to happen.

As they struggled to save their lives. Help did come . . . but it came from those in the afterlife. Things began to change and happen that no one in anyway believe . . . not even Johnathan.

In the time of a mans darkness and a mess, he must learn through his rivalry that he will never stand alone, that if he looks behind him . . . he finds, there is; a Calvary.

Frank Mathis

Dedicated to my wife Wanda, who helped to make sure
this story was finished.
Also to my son Jonathan, who also seen my dream finished.

Chapter One

As an early June morning was rising and the sound; of life began to stir, so was Johnathan Olson. The seven-teen year old star batter for Baxter High. Most of the girls there had their eyes on him for sometime. He was a very good looking lad from Portland, Maine, where the winter was very cold and summer was average. His not so long brown hair and grey eyes and well tanned body, got to them. Rolling out from bed, he made his way to his dresser to do his morning check on his face, making so sure that he didn't have any acne showing. He was the only child living with his mother in a small two story house not far from town where she worked for a floral company. She was a slim woman, age thirty nine with dark brown hair. The sad thing about her was that she was a widow. Her husband was killed by a drunken driver seven years earlier, but she still loves him still. Johnathan got dressed and headed downstairs to get breakfast, boy was he hungry for something good to eat. He knew it a gonna be a busy day and he needed all the nourishment he could get for it. He took his seat and began fixing his plate when his mother looked at him and asked,

"'School Is almost over, what do you plan on doing, maybe for the summer?"

"Don't really know right off, maybe getting a job while schools out I guess."

"Isn't Mr. Garfield hiring anyone to help him at the market this summer?"

"Maybe, I'm—going by there after school let's out, see if he's gonna hire anyone."

As—he gathered his things he needed to take along, he turned to his mother, and gave her a quick kiss on her right cheek, and: left out the front door for not too long journey for school.

Johnathan enjoyed his walks to school each day he went. He loved the scenery that only Portland had to offer anyone who lived there. The mild spring breeze was so refreshing, and the trees just sway slowly side to side. Just up ahead of him, Brian and Arnold were walking together for school. They seem to be in one of their heavy conversations as usual, could be planning on what they might do when school lets out for the—summer.

"Hey you guys! Wait up, let me catch up with you". Johnathan took off in a gallop to catch up.

"Well, well, well, it's Portland's all-star," Arnold said with a big breathily laugh.

As Johnathan caught up and came to stop at the side of Brian, he laid his right on his left shoulder, "What you've two got going on this lovely morning?"

"Oh, Just trying out some ideas about what we can do while we're out for the summer, what are you going to do?" Brian asked, while crossing his arms to his chest. Both friends of Johnathan's were your average teens, who you'd might say are not so well built into sports. Brian you see is smart and pretty cunning, with blue eyes and has a dirtish blond hair to along with his five foot, six frame. Arnold on the other hand, was a bit shorter, five foot, four inch's, with black hair and brown eyes. Arnold was real good in history class, he wanted to become a teacher one day, and teach history in school.

"Don't know right off, after we get out today, I'm going by the market and see if Mr. Garfield might hire me on for the summer, that is, if he'll hire anyone".

Both Brian and Arnold, looked at each other and rolled their eyes, and shrugged their shoulders, like, "Whatever". Then, Johnathan asked them both, what they think they'll do during summer besides messing around.

They told him that they were going to a summer camp, and work with kids in certain fields. As they kept on walking, they saw Peggy Warner pushing her bike to with books piled in basket on the handlebar. She was the best soccer ball player the school had going, Peggy had long red hair, with green eyes, and had the all American figure to go along with her,

"Peggy, wait up!" they shouted at her.

"Can I help push your bike for you?" Brian asked with a big smile that girls thought was his best feature. "Sure, if you don't" mind pushing it".

"Nope, my pleasure, my pleasure", Brian: replied back to whom he thought of as his dream girl. "What's your plans for the summer, got any?" Arnold asked with happiness.

"Going to Canada with my parents, dad rented a cabin for three weeks, right now, I don't know what they have in store." Sounding not a bit interested.

Soon, they all made it to school, counting down the days they had left till they got out and begin what may become their best summer yet.

Johnathan kept up his studies like he's always did, nothing would stop him from getting a good job later on in life, The three o'clock bell rang, and all the students hurried to leave the grounds.

Fast as he could, Johnathan made his way over to see Mr. Garfield, hopefully filling he would get hired.

"Sorry son, not hiring right now, having to cut back till things get straighten out economic wise, know what I mean?" trying to not hurt Johnathan's feelings.

"Well, if you need someone, you have my number, but thank you for talking with me, I guess I'll be seeing you". Since that's over, Johnathan thought of other things his days out of school, but what?.

Chapter Two

A disappointed Johnathan slowly made his way back home. Seeing his mother taking the mail out of the mailbox. Her dress and hair flowed with the light breeze, so it gave the appearance of a portrait. "How did your day go honey?", Asked his mother.

"Not bad, just did our regular everyday school thing, that's about it, stopped by the market about a job, they're not hiring right now", Johnathan replied a sunken heart kind of way. His mother looked at him with love and a warm smile.

"Don't worry dear, something will come along," Then, she came across a envelope addressed for her son, it was from her way off older brother, Robert. She was only two years younger than him and they both had their dads way, "Here son, a letter from your Uncle Robert, see what he has to say.

"Oh boy, a letter from Uncle Robert", he said breathlessly excited. "Wonder what he's got to say?," as he fumbled to get it opened. He began to read the letter out loud to his mother, the more he read, the more Johnathan: got excited. "Mom, Uncle Robert wants me to come out and spend some time at his farm-ranch in Montana, and have fun and goof around. Says here, there's great fishing and all kinds of hunting, He says here, Chuck wants me to also come, that it's been too long since we've seen each other, that it would be nice to come and have fun with you again, how 'bout it, partner?"

This was a dream come true, to spend part of his summer at his Uncle's farm ranch, how swell it would it be, "What do you say mom, would it be ok to spend a little time with them, I won't get into trouble, can I go?" Sounds like someone wants to go pretty bad

"Can't see why you couldn't go, do you a lot of good to get away, be around some people who care about you do ya' good. I'll be alright, I'll invite my sister to come and stay some, she'll enjoy it," Johnathan's mom looked at him with a very sincere expression, she always wanted him to do good, and tried to let him to make his own mind and to find what interest in what life is. "Thanks mom, I'll get in touch with them, let 'em know you said it would be alright to come visit for a spell!" Johnathan ran in the house to write them a letter, telling them he would be there in about three weeks, when: school was out for summer. When he was through with his letter, he put in a envelope to be mailed the next day.

That evening, after Johnathan and his mother had eaten their supper, he helped his mom clean the few things in the kitchen sin. Soon as all that was all done, they decided to call it a day, Johnathan however, took a little time and go over some of his studies before the next day.

Johnathan met up with Brian and Arnold, and told them of his good news. They thought it was real cool, going that far, a vacation at a farm—ranch, how lucky that someone could get, riding horses, and fishing, also go an do some hunting. They where happy for him, since there wasn't going to be no job at the market.

Later after school let out, Johnathan left for his house. His mother in the meantime, was finishing all that was left of the cleaning in the house.

When Johnathan got home, he gave his mother a little kiss on her right cheek. "Did everything go well in school today son?" she asked putting away her dust cloth,

"Yeah, couldn't ask for no better. Did you give my letter to the mailman, for me while I was in school?" "Yes, "and your uncle Robert should get it, next week, if the mall service runs the way it suppose to." His mother sounding hopeful about it all.

Then, with a big long stretch, Johnathan asked his mom , what they were having for supper.

"Well, I'd say, whatever throws its hind legs up, but, how about us eating out for a change, how's that sound?" His mother replied jokingly with her sly looking smile.

With his eye's looking a bit wide, he agreed, a lot better than lord knows what would throw its hind legs up.

Later that evening, both of them just walked around the town and looking in a few shopping stores, picking out things one or the other thought, might look good in the house, "Time we'd better be heading back home," His mother said, taking a quick look at her watch. "Need to finish a few things before turning in for bed," "Well, I've got a little studying I need to do also, before I turn in," Johnathan said to his mother, as it was something he dreaded to do. When they finally got back home, they set their own way getting done what had to be done, before it got late.

As they got started on their work, the phone began to ring. "Johnathan, it's Brian." His mother called up to him. Johnathan picked up his phone beside his bed, "Brian, what's up?" He asked, letting out a small sigh.

"Thought I'd give you a buzz for a few minutes, nothing much to do after I did what studying I had to do, what have you've got going ol' chum?" Brian asked, sounding bored,

"Hitting the books myself, want to get done before too late, need to get some sleep soon, so talk fast." Trying-not to sound rude to him.

"The main reason I called is, if you go visit your uncles place, how long you'll be gone?" Brian asked, as if he had concern for his leaving.

"Don't really know right now, two weeks, maybe three at most, I don't want to leave mom too long, even if her sister does come and stay while I'm gone, you know how she'll worry most of the time." Johnathan told Brian, having great love for her, "I need to get off the phone 1 have to get this studying done, or else, see ya' tomorrow o.k.? bye." Then he grabbed his books to get down into studying for school the next day.

Chapter Three

When the next morning had arrived, Johnathan's mother nearly had breakfast almost done, just waiting for the toast to pop up. She soon made her way to the stairway and let him know that it was time to eat.

"Johnathan, it's time to eat, come on." She made her soft toned voice heard. Just a few minutes later, her son made his way to the table, and his appetite too. He was in the best of a good mood, two days left when school would soon be out for the summer.

"Good breakfast mom, better hit the road, I want to try and catch up with the guys before it's too late." Grabbing his things, he gave his mother a quick peck on her right cheek, and off he went.

It didn't take him long, when he saw the other two up ahead of him. Johnathan came up to the side of his friends, and gave them both his biggest smile.

"Nice day this morning, too bad we have to wastes it on all our classes, right?" jokingly asking them.

"Say, who died and made you mister sunshine, who?" Arnold returned, looking as though he didn't get too much sleep at all. "Just think good men, only two days left, and we're free to roam wherever we please." Johnathan said looking—up toward the blue sky, still a smiling.

Arnold explained to them, why he didn't get to bed till late. Soon the other two cut him some slack, for-them, it was better him, not them.

When the bell finally did ring, all three boys met up to stop at their favorite place for a good soda pop.

When they got to the soda shop, they all asked Andy who helped run the places to give them what they liked.

As they began to drink their sodas, Peggy pulled up to the front, got off her bike and pushed down her kickstand. She too joined them in a refreshing soda.

"What are you going to do when you leave here, if I'm sounding too nosey?" Brian asked, fixing to take a swallow out of his bottle.

"Don't know right off, help mom out for awhile, I guess. She replied, moving her straw up and down in her glass, "Well Johnathan, you still thinking of going to spend part of summer at your Uncles place?" Peggy asked him with her left hand moving her hair to the side.

"Sure I'm going, can't get a job to make money, so since you all are going away, now I'll go somewhere." They just looked at him for awhile, then they finished up their sodas and soon left.

On their way going home, the guys were pitching a baseball to one another. Arnold being silly, threw the baseball over Peggy's head, almost making her fall off her bike. After messing around, Johnathan left them to head on home.

He was so happy that now, he was going to spend some well worth time at a place he's never been to, and was looking forwards to going there on his Uncle Robert's ranch. As he soon got home, he smelled something very good, it was fried chicken, his favorite.

"Sure smells good, I'm about starved, how soon do we eat, if I may ask?" being so polite.

"In about ten more minutes, go and wash up, it'll be almost ready," She told him as he went to clean up.

After they had eaten supper, both of them cleaned the dishes and watched some television for a couple of hours.

Johnathan got up out of the recliner, told his mother he was going to study for awhile, then would turn in for the night. She said that she was going to sew a little while, and go to bed herself. He mentioned how good supper was, gave her a peck on her cheek and started up to his bedroom. When he got in his room, the phone began ringing this time it for his mother. So Johnathan made himself abi relaxed, and started to study for the next day.

Chapter Four

Finally, the big day came, school was out for the summer. Everyone was so happy, so much screaming and going on, Johnathan and his friends took off to their hangout for a good soda to celebrate.

They all made their salute and started to drink, Arnold took a big gulp, taking a rough swallow, he looked at Johnathan and asked "When do you plan on going to your Uncle's place?"

"Soon as I hear from him, and then make all the arrangements, then I'll know for sure," Johnathan said, looking at what a small swallow he had left in his pop bottle, A half hour later after paying for their sodas, they got their things together, and soon left.

Along the way, the boys got to teasing at Peggy. Poking so much fun, Peggy was laughing so hard, tears began to run at the corner of her eyes, "You guys, I swear, you are crazy, and darn well looney!" She told them, still wiping away her tears of laughing too hard. It had gotten time for them to get on home, All of them parted their way, ready to make their plans for the summer, Johnathan made his way home, to see her moving the yard furniture.

"Wait mom! Let me give you some help, wait!" He yelled to her. He ran a feet, till he made a heavy sigh of breathing from the run. "Here, let me move this stuff for ya', it's a little too heavy for you to move by yourself, let me do it." Johnathan sniffed his nose, than he started pulling' and dragging,

"Got some good news for you," said his mother, as he drug another chair, "Your Uncle Robert called me earlier today, I told him you was looking forwards to come and visit awhile with them, and, guess what?" she paused a

10

few seconds, He's sending you a ticket for the bus ride to Montana, isn't that great news?"

"A bus ticket, oh man, that's real great!? A huge grin suddenly appeared on his face. "Whew will Uncle Robert send it to me?" he asked nearly spinning around.

With her prettiest smile, she said, "tomorrow, first thing, you'll get sometime next week," She was so very proud, that that her son was going to finally, have a vacation he'll always remember.

"Now, I need to get in that kitchen, and get our supper started, I'm getting a bit on the hungry side, I think I've had enough excitement for the day." So off she went to get things started.

Johnathan in the meantime, moved the last two wooden chairs nearer to the matching table, the way she wanted, Johnathan was so happy, he rushed in the house, and started calling his friends, and give them his good news. They each were so glad for him, getting to spend time, doing neat things better than what was waiting for them. His mother soon called him, that supper was ready.

After they had eaten, and they both cleaned up, he went to the book shelf to get an encyclopedia book to look up on some facts about Montana, and their ways of living. He was amazed, of what it had to offer. After he read and studied on the state, Johnathan got more and more excited about going, then it dawned on him, how about his mother's sister, will she come and stay with her while he's gone? He thought he'd better find out, before it was too late. He soon approached her, he was very worried, he didn't won't her to be left alone.

"Mom, are you going to call Aunt Jean, and see if she'll come, and be with you while I'm away?" he ask hoping that she would come.

"Well son, after your Uncle Robert called, I called Aunt Jean. She'll be glad to stay with me, and, she asked if it would be alright, if she could also bring a friend of hers along, I told her, that would be alright by me." That was letting her son know, she was going to be fine, and no need for him to worry.

That made it all better sounding for him, now he could go, and not worry one bit for her, she'll have plenty of company. "Great!" he thought, "Just great!"

When Johnathan went to bed, his mind began to stray, wondering of all the fun he'll be having, and what he and his Cousin Chuck will do together. He turned over on his side, the stars were big and very bright. He laid there, staring, till his eyes got heavy, suddenly, he went into a deep sleep, tomorrow another day.

Chapter Five

It was now the third week into June, since school let out for the summer. The weather in Portland, Maine, was getting very comfortable for everyone, especially the folks who worked around the Harbor.

Johnathan and his mother, would walk down there to pick up some good 'ol fresh fish, that hadn't been too long caught, Johnathan was learning from his mother which fish was good, and which wasn't good to buy.

For both of them, it was always an adventure just rouse about the town, see inside the stores, and to check up on what the summer styles are in this year. Haring so much fun together just being out, many times his mother wished that it would be good if her husband could be with them, and share all their happiness they were having, but, she knew deep down in her soul that he was with them in spirit. She brushed away a tear from the corner or her left eye, then looking at her watch, it was soon time to be heading home.

Along the way, they waved to all that knew them, even Mr. Garfield, who was heading for the bank.

After they had made it back home, they started to put everything away, "How does fish and hushpuppies hit you for supper?" she asked Johnathan, as she was closing a cabinet door. "Sounds good too me, nothing like some fresh fish, and good 'ol hushpuppies, makes it all the worthwhile waiting for," as he looked toward the kitchen ceiling, with big delight.

Johnathan, later went to check the mailbox, to see if they had gotten anything in the mail. Two for his mother and a thick envelope for him, it was the one he had been waiting for, it was from his Uncle Robert, He made a dash to the house. He nearly felled to the floor, trying to get in the kitchen where his mother was.

"It came, the letter came front Uncle Robert!" he was so excited, hollering, and carrying on.

"Great! Open it, and read it too me, o.k.?" she asked him, beings polite about it.

"O.K.! Let me get it open, it so thick," he was having a rough go of it, he handed the letter to his mother, "Here! You get it open, I am too nervous to do it."

Boy, and how he ever was, she took the envelope, and took a sharp kitchen and slid it through the sealed envelope slowly pushing it in so no damage would be done to the letter inside. When she had finished opening it, she handed it back to him, Johnathan pulled the letter out, and sure enough, there it was, his bus ticket!!

Johnathan's lips began moving, but, in silence. So his mother, looked at him for a few seconds, then she soon spoke up, "Son, are you going to share your good news with your dear 'ol mother?" she sweetly asked him.

"Oh! Sorry, I didn't think, here! Listen what Uncle Robert has too say," Johnathan started over, reading: all the things that they would be doing, and had gotten his letter, three days after he had called, and spoken about him coming, and have a real good time with him and his son, Chuck. When he had finished; reading his letter, he had the biggest grin on his face, and for his mother, it was the best that she'd let him go spend sometime with her sweet far off brother, and his cousin he hadn't seen since his father's funeral. She stood up, and gave her son a big hug, she was so proud of him, deep in the bottom of her heart, she was going to miss him.

Turning toward the refrigerator, she told her son, "I hate busting your bubble, but, I need to get supper on, or go to bed hungry, you wouldn't want that, do you?"

Johnathan didn't like that idea, going off to bed and not having eaten any fish, and hushpuppies, a very bad idea at that. While his mother was cooking, he called up all his friends, telling them his good news. They were, well, what you'd say, envious of him. But, he needed to spend a little time with his family, no matter how far he'd have to go. The big question they all asked was, when will he'd be leaving? He told them, as soon as his Aunt Jean got there, making sure his mother would be alright before he would leave on the bus. That was the way he wanted it to be, or, he wouldn't go at all.

Chapter Six

Trash day had come, Johnathan grabbed all the bags he had, piled next to the storage shed. Six bags and three old beat up chairs, "Well, that's, that", he said to himself, looking at all the stuff he sat out. So Johnathan decided that he would take a breather for a few minutes, so he sat down on one chair that seemed more sturdy.

Looking around the yard and the house, he was having thoughts on what he'd do next just to pass the time.

Suddenly, he heard a strange sound, sitting his sight on what was coming up the road. It was an old '62 Ford Station wagon, He could see steam coming out from the hood, sounding as though it was on its last leg. From where he sat, Johnathan couldn't see who was driving it. As the station wagon made its way closer, he barely could make out the two figures in it. The red and white vehicle aimed it's way into their driveway, and sputtered to a halt, Johnathan stood up, a huge grin filled his face, it was his Aunt Jean. Both women got out, he saw them laughing pretty hard, each one was wiping the tears that was running down the corner of their eyes. Johnathan, he too began laughing at the sight of the two.

His mother was just starting up her second wash load, while all this laughing was going on.

"Aunt Jean, you are a sight for sore eyes, and I, I mean a sight, come on, mom will be so happy to see that you made it, before "old faithful" gave out on you," he said, as he was trying to control his laughing, as he started leading them to the house.

"Mom, mom, Aunt Jean, and her friend, they're here, I say, they're here!" he shouted in great excitement.

His mother entered into the living room, as she wiped her hands on her apron, tears of joy slid slowly from her eyes. "Jean! Oh Jean! How good of you to come, I hope I didn't take you away from anything important, I trust?"

She asked, looking so happy, not seeing her sister, for almost two and a half years.

"No-o-o dear one, I've been: dying to have a good excuse, just get out of that drab house of mine, knowing I'd be better off spending more time with you, since, I guess Johnathan was going to be gone awhile." She made a little face at him, all in good jest. "Oh! I want to introduce a dear friend of mine to you, this here is Ellie, Ellie Yearwood, she's also a widow."

"Oh! I'm . . ." trying her best to be—so sincere, "I'm, so sorry, looks as though we're in the . . . same boat, I, guess," she said, giving a quick smile and, rolling both her hands on her apron.

Mrs. Yearwood, on the other hand, just nodded her head in acceptance, and smiled. Aunt Jean was delighted to see her sister, Wanda, she then asked.

"Would it be too much, to talk around the kitchen table? I do like some coffee, and you El lie?"

"Sure! I'd love a cup," Ellie agreed, with a wide smile. They all went into the kitchen, both women pulled out a chair and sat down, while both Johnathan and his mother got the cups, and they then sat down and resumed talking with their guest. "Well Johnathan, when do you plan to leave?" his Aunt asked, then taking a sip of coffee.

"I called the bus station, and there's a bus leaving out Saturday, but, I'll switch buses three different times, I should be get there, Thursday." "Boy!! you'll need two days rest, going that far, I'm still tired just driving from Bangor."

"Maybe, it wouldn't be so bad, if we should go the scenic route, their I could see places I saw only in my text books." Johnathan said, as he was getting up, and get some more milk, and a piece of toast. After he'd' taken a bite, and took a swallow of his milk, he then told them, "I need to call Uncle Robert, and let him know, that I'll be leaving this Saturday." When he finished, Johnathan got up, and he went into the living room to call his Uncle. "Wanda, you still keep a—lovely, clean house. I know I'm only thirty six, and divorced, it takes me days to get my place, to look as good as your home." Aunt Jean told her sister, admiring all the nice things that her older sister had, that was only the kitchen, she thought it would be nice, and see the rest of the house. So, they all got up from the table, and the tour, began.

Chapter Seven

Saturday morning had finally arrived. Johnathan was awakened, by the sound of breakfast cooking.

Slowly turning over, he looked at his clock, with a few blinks, he saw that it almost eight O' clock, helping himself to a few more minutes of sleep, Johnathan decided it was time to get on up. When he had gotten dressed, he made his way downstairs to the kitchen, and got a cup from the cabinet and fixed himself a good-morning cup of coffee. His mother and Aunt Jean, was just about finished with the breakfast, when Ellie still a little bit sleepy, walked in and said her good-day to everyone.

"My, my! The breakfast sure does smell wonderful". Ellie said, sounding more perky than the day she and his Aunt arrived. Soon, they all gathered around the kitchen table, Aunt Jean gave the blessing, when she through, they began to eat. His mother spoke to him about his trip to Montana, asking him to please call when he got there o.k. Half of her was happy about her son going on this trip, the other side, she felt sad, but it was her late husbands brother, and it was nice to think of Johnathan and let him come and visit with them for awhile. As his mother, swallowing with care was getting ready to speak, his Aunt aware of what his mother was doing, interrupted to say a few words in his behalf.

"Dear, if this is his first time being away, let him leave in peace, Ellie and I will be here without any problems, isn't that right Ellie?" trying so hard to convince her sister, that he needed time away, and that he was old enough to do this trip on his own. "Son, if you need any help with anything, just let me know, o.k.?" His mother was feeling much better, so much better, that, she

19

had her son call his friends to come over for a little while, a nice little send off. "Say son, where is the camera? We can take, ah, some pictures before you have to be down at the, ah, Bus Station, alright?" She asked her son, still deep down inside, she wanted to keep him at home, but why spoil his summer, Johnathan and Chuck were so close when they were younger, now he'll get with him again, Lord knows what they'll get into. Her sister and Ellie, got some refreshments and a cake, time was getting on, so after everyone arrived, all of them were giving Johnathan their best, wishing it was them and not him, but, it's not everyday someone gets a chance to go to a place such as Montana, that's a dream come true.

Peggy approached Johnathan, giving him the look one would see in a movies "Johnathan, I want you to take this lucky coin with you, it was good to me all through school, I want you to take this along with you, I figure you could use it, o.k.?" Peggy's eyes seemed so solemn, that you could tell she was trying to hold hack a tear.

Arnold and Brian also had something for him to take along, a picture of them that was taken at soda shop before school was out.

"Here, if you get lonesome, you can always look at this, we'll be with you, no matter where you are, we'll be there, right ol' pal?" both of them gave the same look as Peggy, but with their prankish kind of smile.

"Look you guys," his Aunt said, trying to do what she does best, lighten things up. "he's going to visit for a few days, he's not, like, leaving Portland forever, it's nice he has a chance to get away, see the places he's only seen in books, give him a new outlook on life, right?" They all began to cheer up, she was right, the boy needed sometime away, see how the other side lived, and to explore new areas and learn. It was near time for Johnathan to leave, it was a hectic moment, getting his suitcases gathered together and getting in his Aunt's car. It didn't take too long for them to get to the station, once they'd gotten there, they began saying their goodbyes, they were all hugging him and kissing, the guys they just shook hands. When he had boarded the bus and got seated, he started waving at the small crowd, Peggy, in her funny way, blew him a kiss, then she moved her mouth telling him to be careful. The bus made a jerking motion, it was pulling out, Johnathan was on his way, going on his long journey for Montana.

Chapter Eight

IT had been two days, that Johnathan has now spent, riding on the bus. Already, they had stopped three different times for a passenger change over. So far to date, he's met with all kinds of people with different occupations, some he's never ever heard of. On the third day of his trip, they had a two hour delay to change to a different bus. After everyone had gotten aboard, Johnathan decided it was time for a nap, so as the bus pulled from the Illinois Bus Depot, he made himself comfortable, took one more look out the window, then closing his eyes, he was snoozing away. When—they came into the state of Iowa, he perked up a bit, wanting to see what good sites it had to offer.

A man sitting next to him, began a friendly talk, that he'll be getting off at Claxton, he has a small business there with a brother and two sisters. Their specialty was Oats and Soybeans, and now and there, they might take a notion and deal around with a little bit in poultry. This really held his interest, till it was time for him to get off at his destination, in about one hour.

The nice gentleman, politely introduced himself as Mr. Harold C. Kenny, of Kenny Farms, it has been in the family for over fifty three years, Johnathan was overwhelmed with the history of it's beginnings, and how much pain and blood went in to make it what it is today, and they'll keep on running it till the last one dies, cause all of them was a fighting member, "Yep, when our Dad got real bad off, and couldn't do the things he loved doing, the rest of us started pitching in, we all learned what it took to run a business and I must say, we've did one hell of a job to keep it going, to know what was coming and what was going, after he died a while back, the family and I took complete control so we wouldn't lose it, the farm was our home, and that was the way it was gonna stay, till all of the rest of us joined him." The man had spoken, and spoke with great pride, then it neared the time to get off at his stop, he bid Johnathan farewell and a lot of luck, the bus pulled in, soon, he was off.

Johnathan, hearing of a twenty minutes layover, got off just long enough to grab a soft drink, a bag of chips, and a cheap magazine to read. When he had gotten back on his Bus, they announced that in three minutes they would soon pull out.

When he got back to his seat, someone was already sitting in his place. Johnathan looked a little stunned at what seemed to be, one of the prettiest girl he has ever met, next to Peggy. Her hair, it was sort of a dirty blond, her eyes was like sort of a brownish color, and, she had a real good shape to go along with her. The smile she had, would make any guy melt to any level. As Johnathan just stood and admired the young girl, in a soft low tone she started speaking to him,

"If I've gotten your seat, I'll move to another seat, and you can have this one back," It was hard for Johnathan to say anything except, the right thing. Still looking her over, staring at her near shoulder length hair and her eyes. "Well, do you want me to move, or, stay seated?"

"No! No, you can sit there, it's like, nobody's name is on it, right? So please, stay, I'd love to have someone around my age to talk with for a change, that is, if you would like talking to a stranger." The Bus began to move out, Johnathan sat down real quick, the jarring motion made him sway a little to the right, that's what made him sit.

"Glad meeting you, I'm Johnathan Olson, who, ahh, might you be?" Johnathan was still struck by this girl who he thought, looked like an angel, that fell from the heavens, and landed in his seat.

"I'm Iris, Iris Simmons, on my way to Montana, going to visit some kin folks I'd hadn't saw over a good many years, where might be heading for?" She was giving him that look, as though asking the big question, "What you doing tonight you stud?" "Going to Montana also, going to stay at my

Uncle Roberts place for awhile, not for sure how long, but it's going to be fun, staying on a ranch farm, it's like a dream come true, first time I've ever for me being outside my hometown in Portland, in Maine that is." Iris right off could tell, that Johnathan was a bit nervous, the way he was moving his hands, and picking at them. She turned facing him, with her on seductive way, she started talking of her trip also, "That's so weird, both of us going to the same State, I'm also going to stay on a ranch, but, I don't think they have a farm." She was reaching in her pocketbook, putting her hand in it, she pulled a stick of gum out, taking it out the wrapper, she put it in her mouth and began to chew on it.

"What I look forwards to, is horseback riding, have you ever been on a horse before?" she asked in excitement of riding on horses.

"One time only, it was at a friend of mines Birthday party where I was about seven, I wanted to ride it forever, but mom thought two hours was long enough, that!, was the first and last time I've been on a horse, I'm a western fan, so that might help me to get back in the spirit of riding one again."

As he finished talking, he saw dark clouds off their left side. "Looks like we maybe getting rain."

He remarked, showing somewhat concerned of what was heading their way. Iris on the other hand, thought this would be a good chance to grab some shuteye, she was so tired from her day at the Bus Depot waiting to board it. Johnathan, eating what little he wanted, also thought taking a nap would help break the boring ride down a little, since he's been on it a lot longer than Iris. It was an hour and a few minutes later, the rain started to come down, boy, did it ever.

Iris soon woke up, greeted by one huge flash of a lightening bolt, then, a loud sound of thunder, that one would think they were under attack by enemy fire. She threw herself sideways, toward Johnathan, while he was in process of waking up. He put his right hand on her shoulder, as she had a bad frightful look across her face. "You o.k.?, I thought for a second there, you was about to go through the roof," Johnathan asked her trying his best not sounding scared himself.

"Yeah!, I'm fine, it's that, I've never heard thunder so loud like that before." Iris replied to him, "If you want, we can trade seats, that is, if you want to," Johnathan was doing his best, showing so much concern for her well being.

Then at that moment, the driver of the Greyhound made an announcement on the speaker, "Sorry for that loud boom, storms like this isn't too rare in this part of the country, weather such as this one, may last, well, I'd say, till we leave Iowa sometime in the morning, so, just relax, and enjoy your trip, thank you for a wonderful trip, and going Greyhound."

"Say!, you didn't answer my question, do you want to switch seats?'" Johnathan asked her once again.

"Nah!, I'll be alright, now that I'm awake. I'll be just fine, it just caught me off guard, that's all." For a split second there, he thought he was getting close to having his seat back, so he gave up, thinking, "What the heck, it's only a seat, nothing more."

It has been a good many hours, when the next day appeared. As some of the passengers was beginning to awake, they heard the driver come on the speaker again. "Good morning to each one, just a little over an hour ago, we came into the great state of South Dakota, even though we had rough rain, we are still a making good timing, so, enjoy your trip and the sights, we will be making a stop in about three hours and take a break, and get things situated, it should take only an hour at most, maybe you'll want to get refreshed, or get a bite to eat if you like, thank you." Johnathan thought, getting a fresh soda and maybe a burger. So he decided to check his funds and make sure he had plenty of money. Taking his wallet out of his back pocket, he counted up sixty six dollars, more than what he'd expected having. When the Bus made it's way to the station, he got up to stretch out a bit.

Are you going to get off, maybe get to see what's going on?" asking Iris, out of being polite,

"Guess I should, get some fresh makeup on, I really need some, know what I mean?" Both of them got off the Bus, Johnathan reminded her not be too long. He made his way inside to the restaurant area, there, he made his order. Then, he thought of Iris, putting on makeup could take a while, so he asked for another order of what he had gotten, so he went and waited for her back at the Bus.

Finally she came back, looking all freshened up, and ready to get back on.

Chapter Nine

It had so far been along ride for Johnathan, he was now getting restless, and a little cranky. Somehow, he knew that he wasn't made to go on such long journeys, especially busses.

Then it finally came, the driver announced to the passengers, that tomorrow they would be arriving in Montana, sometime late afternoon, for Johnathan, that was good enough for him,

"Well! Looks like our long ride is coming to an end, right!" he looked at Iris with happiness.

"Yeah, can't wait to get to my Uncles, I'm going to take the longest bath in history, know what I mean?" she told him looking him straight in his eyes, as though to hypnotize him.

As they were moving on, the sights got so nice. They stretched their necks as they passed that only one would see and read of in some brochure or their history books. Getting closer their destination to come into Montana, both of them had that way of being happy again as they started out being.

The next day just a little pass noon, they had made it to Montana. Johnathan and Iris gave a big hug to one another as they were now getting closer to come to what became the longest ride that one could ever take.

"If you don't mind me asking, where are you, ah, getting off at?" Iris asked in a sly slow way.

"Clear Water, that's where he lives, or somewhere nearby, I'm not real sure, but they'll be waiting for me when I get there," Johnathan told her not being too sure.

Strange to Iris, she dug into her pocketbook, she found the letter that was sent to her awhile back. She turned toward the window, got the letter out of the envelope, looking at it real good, she also saw the same name that she was heading to, Iris thought how strange it was that they were going to the same place, but different ranches, so it seems that way.

It was around about five as the bus pulled into the Bus Depot that also read "Welcome, Clear Water".

Both teens gave a sigh of relief, their journey now was finally over, they made it to Clear Water.

They gathered all their belongings and began their way off fast. As the two of then made their way getting off the bus, Johnathan heard someone shouting a crazed shout that sounded so familiar, he looked over some to his left, and their was his cousin Chuck, just waving like a madman on a deserted island.

Johnathan returned his wave, and he started at a fast pace to join him. The two boys grabbed one another like old army buddies who never seen each one in years. Chuck's dad, made his way to them after he got through parking the car. "Well! I see you two made it here ok in one piece, how did you two like the trip out here?" He asked with a big smile.

Johnathan and Iris looked at one another, a shocked expression came on both their faces. "How do you, ah, know Iris? She said nothing of knowing you guys," Johnathan asked, still in a state of shock.

"Well, let us help with your things, and, on the way back, you will soon know." His uncle told him.

As they all got back to the car, Johnathan and Iris still had a strange look on their faces, not having a clue of what they were about to hear, or find out.

Chucks dad, helped putting their belongings in the trunk, looked at them with what you might say, a. sheepish looking smile.

"Wait till we get back to the ranch, I think it will take your breath away, won't it dad?" Chuck had so much excitement in him, you couldn't hold him down. Both Johnathan and Iris, were sitting nice and comfortable as Chuck kept going on about the ranch and all the things that would keep them amused, he wanted to also let them meet his friends, the ones he goes to school with, and hangs out with. Chuck's dad began telling them of stories of what the Indians tell, about strange riders who only show up at certain times, to help scare off intruders who wants to do evil unto those who can't fend for themselves. The whole time he was telling them this, their eyes where so wide opened, you would think they were dish platters.

While they were all taken in the beautiful sights of the country, Chuck got excited again where his favorite place came into view. "There she is, the most beautiful lake you'll ever see, at least I think it is." Chuck told them, as if he had a love affair with it. "In a day or two, I'll bring the two of you, and we'll do some humdinger of some fishing, how do you like that as a start, huh?" Chuck asked, looking back at 'em as if his eyes were stuck to the side of his head.

"Sounds good to me, what about you Iris, do you like to fish?" Johnathan looked at her, smiling as to hear what she had to say at that matter, "Naw, I'll let you two guys catch all those deadeye floaters that you want, besides, I'm—allergic to 'em, know what I mean?" Looking at them in a non-thrilling sort of way.

"Too bad, just too, too bad." Johnathan repeating at Iris jokingly at her. So as they drove on, soon a long rail fencing coming into view. "We'll be at the ranch pretty soon, just two more miles more."

Johnathan's Uncle said, he couldn't wait to see their expression when they arrive there. Then, it dawned on him, that his Uncle was to tell what the big secret was about him and Iris both being there, and who she was. "Uncle Robert, what was it that you were going to tell us that me and Iris have in common with one another, can you tell us now?" he asked his Uncle, being somewhat concerned.

"Oh, I almost forgot, Johnathan . . . meet Iris, she is yours and Chucks second cousin, from your mothers side of the family, thought it would be nice to have you kids together again . . . besides, it has been along time since you three seen one another, right?" Looking at them through the rearview mirror. Johnathan began to thinking, of how close he came to falling in love, with a relative?

Chapter Ten

As the car came to a stop near the nice two storied house, Johnathan and Iris was amazed to see its beauty, something from the late turn of the century type of home. There was what a place wouldn't be without, a huge wooden barn. "Well, here we are, bet you two can't wait and get settled in from your long journey." Their Uncle said getting out from his side of the car. When the others had gotten out, they just stood there for a few minutes, it seemed so relaxing, so peaceful. Off to the left of the barn, horses was grazing in not quite ankle high grass, Johnathan turned to Chuck and asked him, "how many of them you have? They sure are beautiful."

"Off hand, we so far have twenty three, Anna over next to the corner fence is about to give birth anytime soon, she's been moody for the past week or so, be glad when she delivers," He told him being so concerned about her.

Everybody gathered all the suitcases from the trunk, and headed to the front porch. When they got to the first step, the front door creaked opened, out came an older man, with greyish thinning hair and had on an apron tied around his small frame of his waist.

"Well, well, well, are these the two that you two's been all worked up on to come and visit for a spell?" He spoke out, as they came up the other few steps onto the wide porch.

"Pete, this here is my nephew Johnathan, and here is my niece Iris, she's a kin from my wife's mother side of the family." He then put his arm around her and gave a little squeeze to his left side. "Hadn't seen these two . . . God, it's, been years." He and Chuck, both gave them a big smile of happiness.

"Go show them where they'll stay upstairs, let 'em get rested and cleaned up, Pete . . . how soon will it be till we eat?" He asked, as if he done worked up a big appetite for eating.

"I'm not a magician, it will be about another hour or so, by the time they get settled in, it will be done," Pete told him, as he rubbed his thin narrow chin, and the other hand on his waist.

"That's sounds good to me, you guys and gal get ready, cause there's going to be a lot of good eating going on, so be ready, ok?" Their uncle told them, a big smile still stretched across his well tanned face.

Later on that evening, they all surrounded the table in the middle of the dinning room. It had a cabinet so out of date, that there wouldn't be another one of it's kind around. Then, there was old pictures hanging on the wall, the kind that looks as though they're watching you at every move you would make, Johnathan was wiping off his mouth and turned to his uncle and said, "Boy! this is the best stew that I have ever eating, that I know didn't come out of a can. How about you Iris?" He asked her, while she was putting more stew in her mouth and stuffing some more small bites of fresh baked cornbread behind it. When she had swallowed her food, she replied to him, "It's the best I've ever eaten in along time, it's delicious, so is the cornbread."

Their uncle Robert then to tell them, "Pete here been with us for many a years, one would say Pete is my caretaker and shall I say . . . like a mother to us, right Pete?" Looking at him and giving a quick wink at him.

"Yeah, if you say so, I maybe sixty one years old, I can out cook any woman in these parts, if you can find one. Even if you did, she'd be ugly as sin itself." He replied back, as if he was getting defensive.

When all of them got their fill, they went and sat on the porch to let their food digest awhile. The boys had to loosen their belts as to take the pressure off of them so they could sit and relax.

"Boy . . . I couldn't eat another bite even if you had to use a plunger." Chuck told them as he rubbed his stomach, "Sure sleep good tonight I bet." He added.

"Chuck! When you all let your supper settle some, how 'bout showing them around before it gets dark, just to let 'em get to know their way around it, alright with you two?" Chucks father asked him.

"Sure! As soon as I'm able to get up again." Chuck soon replied with a grin, and the look of someone who labor their hard work at the table. A little while later, the three started toward the barn to look around at it. All that was inside of it was the equipment, and a few bags of seeds, that was kept in good order when it came time for use. Iris didn't seem to be too thrilled.

After taking the grand tour of the barn, Chuck saw a chance to show them the few heads of cattle roaming just a ten minutes from where they stood. On their way, Chuck pointed out a rabbits den, then showed them what was told to them, one of the oldest trees in the county. As they got to the big wooden fence that surround the few heads, Chuck gave out aloud whistle to one of the cows grazing with two others, after a second whistle, one of them turned, and came slowly walking over toward their way. "That's Clairabel, she's one of this farms milking cows we have. Last year she helped win a blue ribbon for being the best looking cow there," He told them while rubbing the left side of her head.

"Go ahead, you can pet her, Clairabel just loves being petted on, she seems to have become the family pet, but! . . . we don't mind." Chuck told them with a look of deep affection while stroking around her ear. Soon after spending some time looking at the cows, it was time to head back toward the house.

They all sat in the big living room, going through a bunch of pictures, some looking old, some where taken within the past couple of years. Johnathan looked back to the old picture hanging up on the dining room wall.

"Uncle Bob, who is that man in the blue uniform hanging on the dining room wall?" Johnathan asked with a curious concern to know.

"Yeah, who is he? His eyes look like cold steel just waiting to cut you." Iris too asked, being somewhat spooked out looking at it.

With a slight laugh under his breath, their Uncle leaned toward them, putting his hands together resting them on his lap, "That! Is well . . . . My great Grandfather, Major Thomas Porter. He saw many a great battles in his time. He passed away in the late twenties of old age. They say that he was to go to fight at the little big horn, but his orders were changed, Custer was sent instead." His eyes were looking off to the picture as if he was expecting him to finish the story. The kids took great Interest, Iris shivered for a second or two, knowing what the aftermath turned out being.

The chiming of the clock on the wall, told all them, it was time to turn in for the night.

"Welp! Time for bed, gonna have a big day tomorrow, need to get a goodnights rest, everyone knows who sleeps where, so, off to bed," Chucks dad said as he stood up putting the pictures back up.

"Goodnight dad," Chuck told his father, "we'll go on up, hope you sleep good."

"I don't think they'll be no problems in that department." His father replied back. Both Johnathan and Iris told their uncle goodnight, and again, they thanked him for letting them come and visit them.

"Goodnight you three, see you in the morning," He said, and off they went upstairs for bed.

Chapter Eleven

The night was providing a nice warm breeze, as all of them got settled in. Chuck and Johnathan, slept on a bunk bed, and Iris slept in a single bed, just across the hall from them.

The boys were swapping stories of what they've been doing over the years, and talking of their plan's in future years too. Iris on the other hand, seemed restless for her part. That picture of Major porter, lingered on her mind. The cold look and his hard features, kept her tossing and turning for awhile.

Both of the boys decided to call it a night, and drifted into a good rest. Downstairs at the time, a restful Pete was snoring up a storm, after making his own plans for the next day. Silent was the night, as the horses just walked and grazed in the moist ankle high grass, as the cows did also. Off in the distance in the trees, an owl could be heard, hooting away.

Yep, tomorrow was going to be another day, and everybody and everything needed to rest for another go at it.

While everyone was getting a goodnights rest, dark figures began to roam the grounds. Two of the figures crept around the front porch windows, and two checked out the back and side windows. When all the signs showed that all was cleared, the dirty business started to unfold, what was to come the next morning, would be shocking to the sleeping occupants.

As a new day was coming in with the sun slowly rose from the Eastern side of the hills. Inside the big house, Pete was getting dressed so he could go to the kitchen and get breakfast started. A little while later, the rest would get up and dressed to enjoy a good meal. Johnathan's Uncle came down first to wish Pete a good morning, and turned on the faucet to wash his hands.

Upstairs, the young teens where all dressed and ready to get a good start on what they had planned to do. Gathering around the table smelling the good food, Johnathan's Uncle spoke in a high very spirited tone, "Well, what do you think you all gonna do today that will get your visit worth while?" as he took a sip of coffee from his cup. Chuck soon spoke as he got the first bite of eggs down his throat.

"Well, I thought we'd go check on our livestock, and later, saddle up some horses and go down to the ol' pond to see if the fish started to surface on top. Maybe after that, ride over to Barry's and let these two meet him, he's real neat." Looking all bugged eyed with excitement at what he had planned.

As soon as they were finished with their breakfast, all three thanked Pete for the great breakfast, and was soon out the back door. The sun was very bright, and the morning air was so refreshing and the birds was singing with all they had. When they had gotten halfway between the house and the barn, all three had the coldest shock that hit them real quick.

"My God, who in the world would do such a thing to your place like this?" Asked Iris in a low and bewildered tone of voice.

"Yeah! . . . whoever did this must have been insane." Johnathan replied with horror in his eyes.

"I need to get dad," Chuck said, with such hurt. So Chuck turned, he ran faster than he ever had.

When Chuck had gotten close to the back porch, he began to holler at the top of his lungs.

"Dad! Hey dad, come and see out here, come quick!" His Father and Pete, were in the process of cleaning the table, when they heard Chuck hollering.

Putting things down, both men rushed to the door to see what in the world was all the commotion was.

"Dad!, Pete!, Look what somebody did last night, come quick, hurry!" Chuck was sounded out of breath.

"Son, what's wrong!" his father shouted back at him. As they stepped outside, they both saw the damage that was done during the night. They had never seen such a mess like this before, not even a storm could have done the mess his place was in. Johnathan and Iris slowly and still shocked as the rest, made their way through the trashed out yard. They all gazed at the barn, it didn't look any better. Paint had been thrown and splashed on the outside walls. Soon, they each made their way inside the barn, more damage was done to the farm equipment, and other stuff thrown about in all directions.

They all had the same thought in mind, "Who would do this? . . . and why?"

Later, they made their way to the front of the house. Their expressions didn't get no better. Dark red Paint had also been splashed on the house and painted on the flooring were the words, "We want your land."

Pete looked over to his boss, and with a solemn tone and asked him, "Who in blue blazes would want this land for, now just tell me, who?"

They all looked at him, as he was looking about the property for some kind of answer, "I wouldn't have no clue as to who wants us out of here, not a clue."

Still shocked at the mess, he told them it was a time now to call in the law, and find out who in the world would do such a dirty deed, as this.

Chapter Twelve

"Bob,. looks as though someone not playing too nice of a game with you folks, they want you to get off your own property, for what?" Sheriff Webber asked him, while he toured all the damaged areas on the site.

"That's what I cannot figure out, who would so far as to do something like this, and not leave a single clue, I-I can't believe this, it's a blooming nightmare," Mr. Porter said in a disturbing tone.

Well Bob, all I can do right now is, take some pictures of this mess, and make out a report and see if we can come up with an idea on who had a dirty hand in doing this, I'm sorry for you guys, your all too good a folks to have this going on." So the sheriff walked back to his car, to do what was to be done.

"Pete!." Mr. Porter called over to Pete. "When Sheriff Webber gets through, let's get this mess cleaned up."

Sheriff Webber was a strong man, with his well built frame, and had salt and pepper hair. This good man was six foot three, he didn't feel like playing around.

After he was through with his work, the rest of the bunch began theirs.

It was some time when they had gotten the worst of the worst back to normal. Pete went inside to get some supper started. Mr. Porter and the rest, finished the last bit that needed to be done.

Iris on the other hand, who didn't complain about the dirt she had gotten on her, she was mad, and felt all the hurt and pain that the rest had felt.

Soon, they went inside to get cleaned up, it was time to eat something real good. Mr. Porter thanked each and everyone for their help in cleaning up the place. He looked over to Johnathan and Iris with such a sad but caring look and said to them, "I'm sorry to have you two come all this way out here and have a good time, I want to apologize to the both of you, for what went on . . . I didn't know this was going to happen, and I want to thank you for helping out." Iris nearly in tears, leaned over her plate, and in her gentle told him, "That's alright uncle Bob, we didn't mind, besides of what we did, I think I lost five pounds, how's about that now?" Trying her best not to cry.

"Me too!" Johnathan added with excitement, "I feel a lot better that we all did this together, won't ever have a chance like this again."

After they had finished their supper, Iris slapped her hands on the table and said over to Pete, "I never had anything this good, since you fixed this great supper, me and the guys will clean up, and you and uncle Bob can go and rest up awhile, now get!, shoo!, go on." Iris was just trying her very best to break the sadness surrounding them.

Both men didn't asked questions, they left!, and fast. The three youths began to gather up plates, cups and glasses. As they began to clean up, Iris began to hum a song. "Sounds like someone's in a good mood tonight, think so cuz'?" Chuck asked as they began cleaning.

"Ohh yeah, sounds as though she's up to something, what do you think?" Johnathan asked back.

"I'm just humming, it takes your mind off your problems, besides, I'm in this too, right?" Telling them right off the bat. "The sheriff is going to look into this thing, and find out who's wanting you guys to leave this paradise of a place."

"Yeah, that's what we all want the answers too." Chuck replied, as he began drying the plates.

When they had finished cleaning the kitchen, all three went out to the front and sit for awhile.

Mr. Porter and Pete looked up as they come out the front door and got a place to sit and rest.

Well, got everything cleaned up for you Pete, so now you can rest good that the kitchen is nice and tidy." Iris told him, with one of her big smiles.

As a roar of thunder was heard, Mr. Porter looked upward at the sky saying, "Storm brewing up, maybe tonight, we'll all get a goodnights sleep," But inside, he was worried about tonight. He soon looked at his watch, it was almost nine O'clock, it was getting time to hit the sack as they say.

"Dad, would it be o.k. if we sat out here for awhile, to watch it lightning some?" Chuck asked his Father who was heading inside with Pete, who knew it was his bedtime, "Sure, but don't be up too late," His dad told him, giving a quick wink from his right eye, then he and Pete went in.

As the storm was coming closer, the more it began to lightning much more also. Chuck got to telling the other two, how often rain would come during the summer, and how the strong lightning made the night look like the fourth of July. Iris listening with great interest, finding out more about Montana, Johnathan paid attention also, till he looked off to the hillside off to his left side. At a glimpse of something at the top of the big hill. The wind started to blow a bit more, thunder was getting more louder, the lightening came faster. Chuck kept talking about the storms. As a big streak of lightening flashed, Johnathan caught another glimpse of the hills, this time he got a good look. Another round of lightening flashed, then he saw it again, what appeared to be dark figures on horses, lined up in a small row of ten. Chuck was about to talk more, when he broke in fast. "You two didn't see what was up there on that hill did you?" sounding pretty serious and confused.

"See what on the hill?" Chuck returned to his cousin as lightening flashed on Johnathan's wide eyed expression on his face, "I don't really know, but there was someone or something up on that hill, looked as they were on horses, lined up. You two didn't see them?" He was now sounding like he was getting all worked up on this matter. Both Iris and Chuck, took another look at the hill, when lightening flashed again, they saw nothing, nobody on the hill.

"Sure you hadn't worked too hard, that the sun might have cooked your brain a bit?" Chuck asked with a wide smile on his face. Then, Iris put her two cents in replying, "Yep! You really out did yourself, and with what happened and all, your tired, yeah, I say you need a goodnights rest." Looking at him in a sly way. But Johnathan, he was sticking to his guns, he looked at the top of the hill, then back at the other two and said, "Maybe your right, I am tired, I did over do myself, but it was for the good!" nearly getting all worked up again.

"I don't know about you guys, I'm turning in, are you two ready for bed?" Chuck began to yawn and then stretch out his arms. Iris got up also and began yawning too. Chuck slapped Johnathan on his shoulder, then grabbed the handle on the door and told them, "Tomorrow maybe better, we'll do something fun, right!"

"Sure, clean' up somebody's mess again, I bet." Iris said, with a dreaded expression and smile to go along with it.

Chapter Thirteen

The storm and howling wind were going strong. The house was quiet, the only sound that could be ever heard, was the snoring coming from Chuck. Thunder cracked hard, lightening flashed bigger and brighter, not even it could bring him out of a good sleep. Pete, he was real snuggled up and must of been having a good dream, cause he had one big smile on his face.

Iris was, well lets say, was sleeping alright, but I think that picture downstairs still bothered her, for she would toss and turn every few seconds, the storm didn't wake her not one little bit. Chucks father, slept good, after lying there in bed, trying to think of who done his place like they did, and why they wanted his land. But for Johnathan, he just sat by the window staring out at the hill, thinking about what he thought he had seen. He decided to lay down, it was almost one in the morning, and he needed to get some sleep or he might not feel like doing anything with the rest. Still he didn't feel comfortable about what he saw, soon Johnathan managed to rollover and drift off to sleep.

Daylight soon came, Pete began his routine of fixing breakfast. The aroma of coffee being made, slowly woke Chucks father, he rushed out of bed and gotten dressed. It was nearly eight, when the swell of bacon and sausage, made its way upstairs, and into the bedrooms where the rest were sleeping. Pete opened the oven door, to check on his delicious biscuits, that no one could resist. Mr. Porter, made his way into the kitchen, and reached up to the cabinet and opened the door to get his cup. Pouring his coffee in his cup, he noticed it was still raining, but not like it was when they all went to bed. "Morning Pete, sure do fix a mean breakfast. Did you sleep good with all of that thundering and lightening going on last night?" "Slept like a baby. Did you sleep any?" looking at Mr. Porter as showing deep concern in his wellbeing.

"Well, I did some thinking for a while, but I couldn't come to know terms of why? . . . why someone would do what they did, and not leave a clue," He told him, as he took a good sip of his coffee, giving Pete a puzzled look, "Too bad I didn't hear 'em, that double barrel shotgun would of sprayed their backsides with some good 'ol rock salt, they'd think twice to pull a dirty stunt like that . . . they sure would." Sounding really ticked off. He began to fry up some eggs, and take up the bacon and sausage. It wasn't too long, Chuck and the other two came down to tear into some good breakfast. Chuck stopped Johnathan, looked at him with a real serious expression that Johnathan didn't expect it coming, "Last night, when you said there some people on horses on the hill, were you pulling our legs?" Johnathan spoke up in a low like whisper, "No! I'm sure there was some people up there, I wouldn't kid about that, after what's happening now . . . maybe after we eat breakfast, we ought to let your dad know, in case, if they show up again, right!" He told cousin, putting a firm hand on his shoulder.

"Yeah, your right, we should let him sure know, in case someone was up there watching us, lets go eat, I'm hungry!" So the boys, joined the others at the table for a good breakfast. They, motioning at Iris, not to say anything about last night, to just hold off till after they've had eaten. She understood, they would wait later.

"Everyone sleep well last night?" Mr. Porter asked them as they reached from plate to plate, getting whatever was in site. "I slept fine, after that storm died down some," Iris told him with a perky smile. The boys agreed together, they slept real good also. Chuck took a quick glance out the kitchen window, saw that it was still raining some, "is it going to do this all day?" sounding a bit let down.

"The weatherman said, that we could have some light rain most of the day." Pete told him reaching over to get another biscuit from the tray in the center of the table. "Well . . . did he say for how long?" "He did." Said Pete, as he put some honey on his biscuit. "Well . . . for how long?" Chuck asked again. Pete was busy chewing on his biscuit when he swallowed it down, he looked at Chuck and said back to him, "till it quits!" Chuck blinked his eyes so quick, everyone began laughing real hard at him, it beat anything he had ever heard.

After a good breakfast, Mr. Porter and the boys, went out on the porch to stretch their legs a while. Iris on the other hand, stayed in the kitchen, and give Pete some help in cleaning up the plates and all, she knew what was coming. Pete tapped her on top of her head, and told her it was nice of her helping him out in the kitchen.

The boys gave Mr. Porter, time to sit down and get unwind a bit, before telling hint about last night.

Johnathan looked at Chuck, and he looked back at his cousin, thinking it was better now, than never.

"Dad, what would you say, if I was to tell you that . . . someone was on top of that hill during the storm last night?" Chuck asked his dad, almost scared that he would be skeptical at him as usual.

"Someone was on that hill . . . in that storm? Who in their right mind, be out in that kind of weather?"

"Don't ask me, Johnathan seen 'em, didn't you say there was a few of 'em up there . . . on horses?"

"Yes . . . I'm sure there was some people up there." Looking his uncle in the eyes.

"What were they doing, anything?" his uncle replied back to him, now being in great concern.

"Nothing . . . they were sitting there one minute, next thing, they were gone, that's all I saw. I thought you needed to know, so you can be on the watch, in case they should return again tonight, or whenever."

Mr. Porter began to believe him, cause deep in his a very mind, he saw this kind of thing . . . before.

Chapter Fourteen

It was heading toward the afternoon, Mr. Porter got to thinking of what was seen. It had been,. well, some time since first setting eyes on them. So, then he decided that taking everyone into town, might help to put him back at ease. He got everyone to cleanup, and go into town for a spell. It would give Johnathan and Iris a chance to have a good look around their town for a change.

When the town came into view, Johnathan and Iris, seen that it didn't seem so big as they'd thought, Mr. Porter saw a good parking space just a few feet ahead.

Where he pulled up to it, Chuck got out to help him back into it. With a big truck as he had, it was going to take a while, to get it parked in the parking space. When he did finally get it parked, they all got out and stood looking around about them.

"Nice town, not too big, and not too small, its so, cute!" Iris being so excited looking about her.

Johnathan, well a nice good looking girl come a slowly walking toward them, he couldn't take his eyes off her, and the others couldn't take their eyes off him.

"If there were ever a lovesick puppy, your looking at him, pitiful, Just pitiful." Pete told them, with a smile of enjoyment at such a site. Johnathan turned to Pete, with a big grin said, "Well! . . . what else could I do, not look at her?" he asked, looking upward toward the sky. "Let's go you guys, we need to be moving on, got some site seeing to do," Mr. Porter reminded them, then he turned away from them, not letting them see him laughing.

They were having a great time. Looking in stores, and checking out historic buildings, they even watched runners take off in a race. Then, the rain started to come down again, so they rushed to get back to the truck before they all got real wet. As they gotten in, Chuck helped his dad to get out of the parking space. When they were all in, they drove away kind of slow.

"How did you like the town?" Mr. Porter asked Iris and Johnathan, sitting in the backseat, looking out at the people heading for cover. "It's real nice, also the folks seem real nice too." Iris said, smiling back.

"Yeah! It's a nice place for one to settle down in." Johnathan replied back, gazing out as to get another look at that girl when they came into town.

They took their time, the rain got a bit heavy in some spots, so no need to rush back.

But, somewhere in a slightly lit room in a building across town, a dark figure is giving some mean looking men some plans to get Mr. Robert Porter off his land . . . and quickly as possible. The dark figure, put his cigar in an oval ashtray and began standing up and started clearing throat, looking them with bounding and determination to get that land and get on with his plans.

"Men, we have got to get that bunch off that land because it's in a good location to build a huge gambling resort and a hotel to pull in some big money and become the richest guys in all of Montana." The guys looked at each other for a second or two, one of them looked back to the big man and he then reply back, "We'll try harder this time around boss, they'll be off that land even if it comes down and killing them, won't we fellows?" Head's began to bob up and down "Then it's clear then, do what needs to get them out of there and soon." The dark figure turned and walked away quietly shutting the door behind him. These guys knew now they need to come up with a plan . . . fast!

When the gang pulled up to the houses they ran up on the porch, to avoid getting too wet as the rain began coming down harder now than when they left from town. They stood on the porch a few minutes, seeing everything seemed in place and hasn't been tampered with. Pete wiped his face off some and said over to Mr. Porter, "I think it looks like a good day we can fix some good ol' soup, I'll go in and get it a started cooking." He looked back out at all the rain coming down and just shook his head and went into the house get started.

"Sorry you guys, didn't get to do much in town, it looks as though this rain is going to stay a while," Mr. Porter said, looking up toward the hills as though he was expecting someone to show up soon.

"That's alright dad, not your fault, if it was to do this, nothing we can do about it, right guys?" Chuck was telling his father, and got the others in it also. Mr. Porter Just looked at them and smiled at them, then turned back looking up at the hills, and noticed daylight was getting somewhat dim.

"I think, that, while you men have some time here, maybe I'll see if Pete could use an extra hand. I can see that I'm outnumbered here as for talking," Iris told them in a low type of voice. She head's inside to the living room area, then the dining area. Iris for some reason, looked up to see that-picture of Mr. Porters spooky great Grandfather, it was watching her. Moving side to side, his deep looking eyes followed her no matter which way she moved. So quickly, she made her way into the kitchen, safe within the site of Pete, just stirring away at his pot of vegetable soup.

"Pete, thought you could use some help, what can I do to help ya' out here?" Iris asked Pete, as she looked back toward the door leading back to the dinning room. That picture sure did give her the creeps.

"Well, you can get some bowls out of the cabinet, and get some spoons from the drawer below it," Pete was so busy, as he told her what to get.

Soon, a loud crack of thunder filled the kitchen, the floor, you could feel the vibration of it.

The guys on the other hand, was starting to come in when they heard someone yell from a distance. They all turned and saw a slim figure just a getting it up the driveway.

"Hey Chuck! Wait!" Yelled the figure on his bicycle. It was his good friend Barry, coming up the drive. He got off his bike and let it fall to the wet ground. He ran up the steps onto the porch, almost out of breath, he pulled his rain hood from his head.

"Boy, what a storm, mind if I could wait here till it slacks off a bit?" He asked, still getting his wind.

"Sure can, what in the world you doing in this wet rain for? Chuck asked him, try to avoid from getting wet while Barry took off his poncho.

"I was down; by the lower field looking around for Dad, when Bam! It began pouring like everything." He explained, grabbing a chair to set in. Then, he took a strong whiff, and said, "smells like your having, ah, soup, right?" That sounds like an invitation coming on.

"Pete's fixing up some, care to have some with us?" Mr. Porter asked him with a big smile.

"Being in that rain as long as I've have . . . sure! Pete makes the best soup, better than anyone that I could ever think of." Barry told them, then he ran his right hard over his mouth, hoping that it wouldn't be too much longer. They all began laughing at him, Mr. Porter put his left hand on Barry's shoulder and with a big grin and told him, "well, if Pete ever heard you saying that . . . I'm afraid he might expect that kind of talk from all of us every time he picks a notion on cooking a meal around here . . . so, don't brag too much." Then he began to chuckle at him.

Iris just got all the bowls and glasses sat on the table, when the fellows came in the kitchen:, Pete was getting through stirring the big pot of soup for the last time. Iris filled all their glasses with tea. The guys each grabbed a chair, and began getting settled in. A loud crash of thunder filled house and made the floor vibration tingled about their feet, they all looked at each other as the thunder faded away, their eyes where about as big as their bowls.

"Sure am glad I'm not out in that storm, it is a sure fire mess," Barry said, as Pete started to fill their bowls with his delicious soup. "Guess dad made his way back home, I know he wouldn't stay out in it no more than an animal would." He said, being concerned that his father got home alright,

"I'm pretty sure he did," said Chuck, after taking a swallow of his tea, "He's a smart person, nobody cares being in that kind of weather, I wouldn't, even if I were starving."

"Now! I've heard it all," Pete jumped in after all the talk he's heard, "The way you put food away, it would be days before you get a rumble in that stomach of yours . . . starving, who are you kidding?" Pete told Chuck, while winking his left eye at Chuck's dad. Soon, more rain, then thunder. Everyone was eating and enjoying their soup, the phone began ringing, Mr. Porter slid away from the table, wondering, who would be calling at this time, when a bad storm is in progress?

"O.K. when this storm has a break in it, maybe I can see you, if it's real important to you.

"Alright then Henry, see you when the first chance I can get, alright, I'll be seeing you . . . yeah, it is a bad one, alright, bye." Mr. Porter headed back into the kitchen, rubbing his lower chin wondering why Mr. Collins needed to see him so, between these two, they never never had what you could call, a friendship.

"Who was it Dad?" Chuck asked his Father, still a bit confused about the phone call.

"It was Henry Collins, says first chance I get, that he needed to talk some important business with me. It puzzles me now, all this time we've lived here, we hardly ever spoke to each other." He looked at Chuck and Pete with raised eyebrows, then he looked over to Iris and Johnathan. Any who, lets finish our soup and I'll go talk to him tomorrow, lets eat.

Now Mr. Collins, was a big figure around town, what you might say is, the big cheese, that owns a great deal of real estate in that part of the country, you could say, he can pull some bad deals if one wasn't aware of what he was offering. Also, he had many men to get what he needed at any cost, to get rid of those who might be in his way.

Chapter Fifteen

When the weather had letup that flowering morning, Mr. Porter, got into his truck, and headed to town in a rush. His mind was going fast, trying to think what was so important, that Mr. Collins wanted to see him about. It seemed so strange too him.

The kids meanwhile, after having their breakfast, went outside to get a look for any damage from the storm. They checked on the cattle, all seemed to be doing what they do best, grazing in the fields, Even Clairabel, who was mostly off to herself, and at anytime give birth to a new calf. All three went back up to the barn, and checked around there for any damage, just a few things blown down, nothing big. Iris walked over to some old crates sitting to a side of the wall. She saw what looked like small leftover cigars. Also, a print of someone's shoes that appeared to have a star-like shape in the middle of it. Iris asked them to come and see. Both boys walked over to take a look, "do you know who smokes these?" she asked Chuck in a soft tone of voice.

"Not dad . . . nor Pete, I sure don't smoke 'em, no telling who's been here that does," Chuck answered back, baffled at the sight.

"Maybe, someone was here at sometime helping your dad out in here," Johnathan replied.

"Nah!, usually it's him and me, nobody else." Chuck a bit confused, said, "I'll ask him when he gets back, he knows most of the ones that smoke that kind."Chuck said, hoping his dad would know. They made their way around the barn, everything else was in its place as always.

It was near one o'clock, when Chucks dad made his way back from his meeting with Mr. Collins, The look on his face, showed he was very upset about something, Pete and the others, made their way to the porch and find out what was said, "Collins, wants to buy this place, he wants to make this a business area, to attract more income to these "neck of the woods" as he puts it. Well, I told him, no way, it's been our land for years, and I'm not going to sell it to anybody, and that's that," he sat down in one of the old rockers on the porch, his eyes began dwell off in the distance and said, "there's something I can do, he's not getting our home, never!" Then Chuck's dad, sat and rocked in the chair looking very mad.

Pete, spoke up to Mr. Porter in an angry tone, "you mean that ol' bag of money wants this land so he can make more money, doesn't add up to me," being truthful.

As for the kids, they, were more or less in a state of shock. All the beauty that surrounds for a lot of miles, and the hard backbone work to make their place what it is . . . a home. But Chuck knew deep down, his father would never give up anything that has been giving to him that belongs in the family. Chuck also thought, one day, it would be his land, having that in mind, he felt what his dad was feeling.

"Uncle Bob, there's no law that a man can give up what he rightfully worked for all his life, to me, I believe a greedy bug got a hold of him," Johnathan told his Uncle, trying to do his part to cheer up his kinfolk. Then, he just thought of those small smoked up cigars, and that one shoeprint that Iris found laying in the barn. He finally decided, this ought to be the time his Uncle may need to see them, it could, or wouldn't mean anything. "Uncle Bob," Johnathan said in his polite manner. "Do you think, you could go out to the barn with us, there's something you should take a look at?"

"Sure! If its important enough to look at, lets go check it out." Johnathan's Uncle replied back at him. Everyone left out, almost in a huddle.

When they arrived inside the barn, the kids pointed to what they had discovered on the ground. "Well, don't know who smokes those, I know their not mine, nor I should say, neither does Pete," Mr. Porter said, looking pretty stunned at all three. "I'd say right off the bat, that whoever the person, or persons where, I might say, were waiting out here when we where in town showing you guys around. Pete! What do you think?" Pete got to rubbing the back of his thin neck in confusion, and went in agreement at what Mr. Porter had come up with.

"Tell you what we can do," Mr. Porter said, when he let out a short breath from his mouth. "We're going to keep a watchful eye, on anyone who smokes these brand of cigars, and, wears shoes with a star on the soles, o.k.?" Everyone agreed at what he asked them to watch for, and they will. As they all turned to go back to the house, Chuck's dad asked, "did Barry makeup his bed and get home alright?" Chuck assured him that he did, and had breakfast too. While walking slowly on back to the house, they noticed the sun was starting to come out, and a patch of blue was coming into view, looks like it might turnout and be a nice day.

When they all got back to the house, Chuck thought about their cow Clairabel, he figured he ought to go and see how she was coming along. So, he and his cousins took off to the field where Clairabel would a been grazing. As they were walking across a shortcut to the field, they were enjoying the cool breeze that was coming from the East, Johnathan looked around the area about him and thought, how this piece of a good land, would make a nice ball field. Iris, on the other hand, took in all the beautiful trees and flowers that nature had to offer. She was starting to fall in love with the farm that she didn't take to at first, now, she started to melt into it.

"There she is! Next to the oak tree." Iris shouted to the other two. Yep, there was Clairabel, eating away, enjoying the warmth of the sun, and the breeze was making her feel so content at what she was doing. Chuck and Johnathan, folded their arms on the gate that kept them safe. "Anytime now, she's going to be a new mother, I know she's going to be glad when all this will be over." Chuck said, just staring at her while she bent her neck downward to pull up a mouth full of good green grass. Chuck soon asked, if they may like to go and check out the pond just aways across the pasture. "I think tomorrow will be great for us to do some good fishing, after while, when we get to the barn, we can gather up all the fishing gear and be ready at early light, how about it?" Chuck began a good convincingly idea to get away from all the problems they've been having so far.

"Sounds good too me." Johnathan replied back to his cousin. As for Iris, she said, that she would take a book along, fishing just wasn't her way of having a good time, so to speak. Two hours later, they were fishing in the pond. As for Iris, she was looking through one of her new up to date teen magazines and borrowed a transistor radio belong to Chuck. The weather was perfect and the small breeze now and then, made it, just right.

"Sure would like to get a hold of the ones in behind to, try and get our land, it just isn't right." Chuck said, like, in a mumbling sort of way. Johnathan, agreed one hundred percent. Mr. Porter has always gone the distance, helping anyone in need, no matter who!

Chapter Sixteen

Mr. Porter and Pete, sat at the dinning room table, to go over the matter with a fine tooth comb, at who would want him to give up his land, that has been his, lets say . . . bread and butter, for as long as he could think so far back, even when his father ran it.

"You know Pete, I'll bet a dollar to a doughnut, Mr. Collins knows a lot more than he's telling me . . . I just have this creepy feeling inside," Mr. Porter sipped a bit more out of his coffee cup, and Pete, he just stared a while at Mr. Porter agreeing with his eyes. Mr. Porter looked up at his great great grandfather's picture hanging in front of him. Looking at his cold steely eyes, he knew he was going to have a fury battle to fight, for him . . . the sooner, the better.

Some hours later, the kids gathered up their stuff, it was time to call it quits. The boys didn't catch nothing, Iris, caught up on the latest teen gossip and styles.

"We'll do better next time, maybe they weren't hungry today." Chuck told his cousins, moving on toward home.

On their way back up the trail, they heard the slamming of car doors. Quickly, they ran to see who it was, but missed them by two minutes. After walking a ways on up the trail, Johnathan, saw some things that nearly took his breath away. He took a step, bent down for a closer intake at what he sees. The other two followed behind him. They too were shocked at what they saw, three sets of good footprints, the print in the middle, stood out real good, it had also the star on it.

"Iris! Run to the house, get dad, he needs to look at this, hurry!" Chuck told her, near breathlessness. The two stayed there, so no one could step on them. When his dad arrived at the spot where they stood and waited, Chuck, a bit nervous. After viewing the prints a few second's, he got up on his feet and looked around the area, Johnathan told his uncle what he heard, but didn't see.

"Let's go to the house. I'll call the sheriff, tell him our intruders made us another visit."

When they got Back, Mr. Porter got on the phone. Telling what the kids had come upon, to come out soon as possible. It didn't take too long for him to get there. They went to where the footprints still was, the sheriff took a while examine the prints, but he couldn't get a clue who they belonged to. He then took pictures of the prints and left.

Mr. Porter and the boys, headed back to the house to grab something to eat. Iris and Pete, were sitting on the front porch, waiting news on what the sheriff had in mind. All three got to the porch, and took a spot and sat down. After a moment of silence, Pete finally asked the big question.

"Well . . . what's he a gonna do about this trespassing that these people are doing . . . what?" Pete was getting pretty fed-up.

Mr. Porter, taking a deep breathy told him that putting some deputies around the place would be the thing that might be the best thing to do. Also, we don't have an idea in the least who's doing all this . . . no one."

The three cousins looked at each other, somewhere they felt all hope would be lost, what could they do, who would they'd be looking for? Knowing their help was in deep need, they knew there, some answers had to come up.

"Lets go watch a little television, it's almost time for my favorite show, The Lone Ranger, let's go watch it, how 'bout it?" Chuck asked the other two.

"Yeah, sounds alright by me." Johnathan replied.

"Beats beating our heads against a wall, count me in." Iris said, knowing she didn't have much of a choice.

Meanwhile, Pete and Mr. Porter, went into the kitchen, to figure out what would be good to fix for supper. Looking in the big freezer, they spotted a big batch of frozen fish. They both agreed, fish and some hushpuppies, maybe a nice big bowl of coleslaw, yum-yum.

The three kids on the other hand, were getting into The Lone Ranger, Chuck told his cousins, that he's been a big fan since he could remember. He told them that a stick horse he had for along time, was named, Silver too. Many hours he would play cowboys and Indians, with some of his friends that now have moved away or don't see much anymore. But now, I was hopeful in making my New Year resolution, this year nineteen sixty five, will be better than before. After the show went off, some cartoons came on.

"If you don't care for these, we can find something else to do," Chuck could see by their expression, they weren't cartoon fans, at all. Chuck there, picked up the idea of pitching some ball till supper was fixed.

Iris, on the other hand, thought she could help Pete in the kitchen some, for what he had started, it was making her awful hungry. So, outdoors went the boys, Iris went to the kitchen to help him out with something. She got taking a fancy to the way of his humor on Chuck and that, he takes concern over the family problems. For her, he's the kind of man to have taking care of her family. As she walked through the dinning room door, she couldn't help to look up at the faded picture of the Majors eyes staring at her. Those eyes she kept looking at, sent cold chills all through her body. Quickly, she moved on into the kitchen, where Pete was thawing out the frozen fish, she waited a few seconds to get herself together.

"Do you need my help with anything, I don't mind." She asked politely. For her, it was better than having that picture staring at her every move.

"Well . . . if you don't mind, you can get that pan over on the stove, and you can spread those hushpuppies in it. We're gonna have to make more tea,

Chuck, he'll go through it like a sponge." He told her, with a quick wink and a small bit of a laugh.

Outside any who, the boys were having a good time throwing some ball to each other. Johnathan, liked this, pitching the ball would help, to keep his good arm in shape.

"How many games has the team your on, won this past year, that you can recall?" Chuck asked, as he threw a curve ball back to his cousin.

Johnathan, caught Chucks hard curve ball, held it for a few seconds and said, "Just this year alone, we won five and lost two, not bad, but the last two, we could of done a lot better, if some of the players hadn't been getting sick." Then he turned to one side, drew back his right arm, and threw the ball as hard as he could.

As for Mr. Porter, he took time just to stretch out on the couch to think, why anyone would try and take away what took his family years to build and hand down for generation to come.

In the kitchen meanwhile, Pete and Iris was having a swell time fixing up a great meal. When Pete puts fish in the big skillet a frying, he knows Chuck will getting his share, if no one can out—eat him. Iris on the other hand, had spread out all the hushpuppies evenly on the big pan, now she was ready to put them in the oven to start baking. Soon, Pete began the process shredding up the cabbage to make the slaw. The aroma started to spread in all directions. When it had made its way to the boys, they knew it wouldn't be too long, it would be time to feast on some good eating.

Chapter Seventeen

Later on in the evening, the three kids went to check on Clairabel before turning in for the night. Chuck gave her the once over, she seemed to be fine, but, she could have a calf at anytime now.

Nine thirty soon rolled around, they soon went up to bed. Everyone still felt a bit full from the supper that it didn't take long falling asleep, until Johnathan awoke. He sat up in bed to look around the room, it looked alright as far as he could see. He went over to the window being quiet, not to wakeup Chuck. Pulling the curtains to a side, he gazed all over the area, nothing moving about, until, he focused his eyes over at the hillside. Their sitting midway, was those dark figures, on horseback, what looked strange this time, they seemed to have moved closer in. Johnathan just stood staring at them, and it looked as though they were staring back at him. He glanced over to his cousin, who, was just a snoring, wouldn't do good to wake him up. He glanced at the hill again, this time, they were gone, Johnathan on the other hand, got a cold shiver running all over him.

All during the night, Johnathan tossed and turned in bed. Those figures kept running in and out of every thought he could shakeout. Every time he'd wake, light didn't seem to come soon enough.

Finally, the daylight broke through, Johnathan gotten up as fast as he could. Pete was in the kitchen making the morning breakfast, and listening to the report on the farming business. "Morning Pete, Uncle Bob up yet?" looking about in a concerned voice.

"Oh yeah, he's up, sounded as though he's been up all during the night," Pete told Johnathan, as he was fixing up some batter for making pancakes,

"Reckon with what's been going on here lately, has him mighty worried . . . but who isn't?" Pete told him with worried eyes, Johnathan went outside to find his Uncle. When he did, he worked his way into telling about seeing those figures upon the hill, this time they were closer than last time. Then, his Uncle spoke, "I saw too, I can't figure it out, whoever they are, they have a reason . . . good or bad, they won't leave until whatever it is, is over with."

"Dad." A voice came in from behind. "I've . . . I've seen them too." Chuck finally got to speak of this. "Been seeing them off 'n on, just never could bring it all out in the open." Chuck just stood solemn, as his dad and cousin stared at him, nothing came to mind from either of them. A couple of minutes passed, his father just winked and smiled at him.

"Well . . . I'm glad to see that we three have something in common, night stalkers," Mr. Porter put both his arms on each boy's shoulders, gave both of them a pat and said, "Lets not say anything for now, unless anyone else has seen 'em besides us," He gave them that, "Lets keep this our secret" kind of look, while looking around them, as not to be seen. Then he told them in a happier tone, "Pete should have breakfast ready by now, how about we go eat?" All agreed and started to the house, mums the word.

As they made their way through the backdoor, the smell of bacon and pancakes welcomed them in for a belly filling time. Chuck got seated next to Iris and Pete, bending just enough over the bacon, getting a good whiff from the bacon dish. Pete took notice, at his sniffing the food. Then, giving a nod and a wink to the rest and shouted out, "If your a going to sniff your food like a dog, go eat with them!" This set everyone to a good laugh, including Chuck.

Meanwhile, back in a somewhat slightly lit building in town, a figure sitting in near darkness, puffing on a cigar and rolling a couple of big marbles, in his right hand. Three other figures stood in the light, waiting to get down to business. Then, the big man as always, pointed his cigar at them saying very gruntly.

"O.K guys, this is the moment I've been waiting on. Tonight, when Mr. Porter and that bunch staying with him goes to bed we're a gonna hit 'em hard.

I want that land, now! Before 'ol man Collins can sweet talk him into selling it to him. So, tonight boys, let's make a real good impression on them and get 'em off that land as fast as we can get 'em off even if we have to shoot somebody . . . do I make myself clear?" He told them, with his eyes piercing them real mean looking. Then, he shoved his half smoked cigar back into his mouth.

"Yes . . . we get you loud and clear boss. But there's something you ought to know . . . we don't want anyone bad hurt, we can't deal with any murder charges hanging over our heads, right guys?" As one: of the oldest spoke out.

"That's right, no bloodshed . . . we'll do anything you want as always boss, but killing, it just isn't our style." The next to the oldest told the head guy. All three looked hard back at him, not saying another word, just staring.

"Alright then, whatever you boys say . . . I guess I'll go along with you, but we need to get them off that land anyway possible, o.k.?" The big boss asked in what seemed a better tone of voice.

Then, one of the boys looking' real puzzled, just had to find out one thing, what was the reason of his wanting that stretch of land so bad, that they would likely get caught and go to prison. "Tell me something boss, if it's alright to be a bit nosey, way does getting that Mr. Porter and them off that place seem so important to ya'?" He asked, putting a toothpick between his teeth. The big figure in the low light, just smiled and said, "when the time comes boys, when* the time comes." That was all he had to say.

As the morning wore on, the kids on the other hand, took to doing some chores outside while it was so nice and cool. The two boys kidded Iris about being cute in her blue jeans and denim jacket.

"One of these days Iris, some handsome guy riding on a horse, will come a galloping along and fall to the ground seeing how pretty you are. Then, he'll get up and run as fast as his legs can go, and he'll a grab ya' to him and plant all kinds of kisses over your lips and face, and then, he picks you up and puts you on his horse and ride away into the sunset," Chuck told her with a big grin spreading across his face.

Iris just stood there, her eyes had that look as if she was about to jump all over him at any giving time. But all she did, was look at the ground and around about her, and she let out to laughing real hard. Then, Johnathan and Chuck joined in with her. Chuck started to make kissing sounds at her, Iris then, gave him a fun smack on his left back shoulder. They soon went about their way, to try and get busy on some things that, it might take most of the day to get it all done.

It wasn't long, that Mr. Porter and Pete, came upon the kids to let them know they had to make a trip into town and get some things needed. "It may take us awhile, just keep your eyes open in case anything comes up, ok?" He told them in his own concerned way.

"We sure will dad, with us here, no one better be up to no good . . . right you guys?" Chuck looking at Iris and Johnathan real hard, to let his father know, that they could handle whatever should rise up. Then, Pete put his two cents in to the warning talk. "And listen you two, keep that food disposal out of the kitchen, I made a cake last night, and, I don't want to come back and find an empty cake plate, ya' hear?" Peter winked at them with his sly smiling way, knowing he was just kidding them.

Mr. Porter than spoke once more, "If anyone should call for me, tell 'em I'll be back as soon as posslble."

Then he and Pete, climbed in the truck, and began their way into town, both waving out the truck.

Turning to Chuck, Johnathan, looked at his cousin with a slight little laugh, and pulling back his hair a bit, then he said to him, "boy, seems to me, he knows you all so well."

"Ahh! Pete's full of Baloney . . . he knows all I can eat is half a cake." Chuck replied back to the other two, throwing one hand in the air and back down again. Iris and Johnathan, both laughed aloud, and began to go back to work on the yard. But for Chuck, a slice of that cake—would go nicely with a good cold glass of milk.

Chapter Eighteen

It wasn't too long, in the day, while the kids on the yard work was nearly done, the wind started picking up fast. Johnathan and Chuck all of a sudden, felt a cold flash come upon them. "Chuck! Johnathan called over at his cousin, "Do you feel that?" Looking around and up and around again, he felt the same as his cousin. Iris still doing what she was doing, glanced over to see the two boys wondering about.

"What are you guys looking for?" Iris asked, as the two boys kept wondering in a circle. "Hey! What are you doing?" Iris asked once more.

"Don't know! something just don't feel right, I . . . I can't figure it out, something is wrong." Johnathan shouted back at her. Minutes later, Chucks father and Pete, pulled up quickly up into the driveway, Pete in such a big hurry, got out from truck, and ran fast as he could, to hurry up and get everything from the back of the truck before the storm hit. "My God! I hadn't seen a storm come up this quick in years.

Mr. Porter had Iris and Johnathan to help with all the bags and anything else that had to go inside. The wind would die down some, then, all of a sudden, pick back up some more. Chuck and his dad, ran to check on all the livestock, and to make sure they would be safe from any kind of harm. After everything was off the truck, the other two ran to where Chuck and his father were, and to lend a hand getting the animals put away in an area near the back of the barn.

"Alright you guys!" Mr. Porter hollered real loud at the top of his lungs. "Better get into the house, this may be with us a while, hurry up!" All three kids rushed toward the house as fast as the wind would let them. As they finally made their way through the kitchen and stopping in the living room, Chuck looked at his cousins with his eyes opened real wide, and then he asked, "did you ever see anything like that in your whole life?" wiping the dirt off his clothes. The other two both agreed, they've never seen a storm come up so fast, what seemed to start as a nice day, then a wind tunnel. Johnathan on the other hand, noticed a figure coming up the drive real fast. They all went out ore the porch holding onto the railings for support from the high wind. They began to squint their eyes to make out who it could be. Iris, as she fought to pull her hair back, saw that it was good ol' Tommy. He made flying leap onto the porch, almost falling on his knees, "What is it about storms that lands you here?" Chuck asked Tommy, as he got to his feet.

"Well . . ." catching his breath, "I was on my way over here while it was still nice, to see if you guys knew about some truck that's been parked down the way of the south field area. I saw it down there yesterday as my Dad and me where passing by from town. Thought someone broke down, or something, that's what I came over for."

But the whole time Tommy was talking to them, he'd glover at Iris, just seeing if she was really taking a notice of his appearance." We saw one the other day, a couple of guys got in it and took off. It might appear that they maybe the ones who messed up our place, only thing is, we don't know for sure who it was," Chuck told him loudly over the rough wind, "Lets inside, it looks like rain coming soon!" They all one by one, went inside to the living room to finish talking some more. It was going on five O'clock, when Pete came in the living room and saw them sitting around talking.

"Well, well, well, that wind must be strong, to land Tommy in here. Maybe . . . he smelt my supper all the way over his house and caught the first tree limb coming this way, right?" Pete said, as he rubbed his chin smiling a devilish look. Then Chuck broke in for Tommy's defense, so he explained what he told them about a truck that they had seen a while back, but they didn't see who was the driver of it. "When did you see it?" Pete asked Tommy.

"When my Dad and me came back from town this morning." Tommy repeated what he told the other three. Then, Pete took a long look outside, it was still rough looking out there. Mr. Porter made his way to where the rest were, and looking about at their expressions on their faces.

"Now what do we have here, a sad face contest, or did the wind blow somebody we know away?" He asked, trying to get someone to laugh, or say something. Mr. Porter then a bit surprised to notice Tommy on the couch next to Iris.

Chuck soon spoke—up, but he didn't want to make it out to be such a big deal, "Tommy was on his; way over to our place, and asked if we know anything about a old truck that looked like it was broke down or stuck down by close to the south field. We've seen one down that area, but we never paid much too it, nor saw who it belonged to. We'd go try and see who's truck it was, but somehow they'd drive off, so whenever we would be in that area, we would keep an eye out for it, right you guys?" They both agreed, and told what else they might have to go along with their cousin's story.

"Well if it spotted again around here, see if you can see a tag number, or any kind of markings to find away of who owns it," The gang all agreed to do better next time they see it there or anywhere nearby. They all felt a big relief, that all this came out now so that when the truck might come back, if ever, they would be better prepared. So, after that bit was done, Chuck got up on his feet and walked over to where Pete was standing, and put his right arm around his shoulders and looked him in the face and asked, "What are we having for this evenings supper Pete ol' boy, ol' pal, ol' buddy of mine?" Peter just looked at Chuck with one of his slick kind of grins of his and stated to him, "Food!" Chucks father and the rest, got a good laugh out of it, and so they began to go about waiting on it.

Chapter Nineteen

The weather started to calm down some-what, it didn't seem as bad now as when it started earlier. They all sat around having a good time just talking and watching some television. It was getting late, so they began to call it a night. Tommy called his parents, to tell 'em that he would spend the night with Chuck and the rest, because it was too rough to try and come home at that time of night. After he hung-up, he headed upstairs to join the other boys.

Pete and Mr. Porter, made their way in the house, to make sure all the doors were good and locked. After a long day, they sat in the kitchen for awhile having one more cup of coffee. Soon, Pete went to his room, and Mr. Porter to his room. The stormy weather sounded good, making it easy for a goodnights sleep. It wasn't long till Mr. Porter, had to get a drink of water. He made his way downstairs pretty good without any lights on, so he wouldn't disturb the other. When he got to the kitchen, he reached his right hand up to find the string that they pull on to get the light on. Then it happened, trying to locate the string, yeah, he found the string and stumped his big toe into the table leg. He then made it to the sink faucet and got a half glass of water, he could hear the wind blowing outside, it didn't sound so bad as when it first started up. Mr. Porter stepped over to the backdoor for a minutes, he opened the door to see if there might be anything that got damaged from the storm. Looking about the place, everything seemed much the same as before.

As he was about to close the door, something caught his attention real quickly. He then ran to the phone to call for help. A deputy on duty answered the call. "Need to get out here fast!" Mr. Porter told the man on the other end,

"What seems to be wrong?" The deputy asked him. "I was looking out the backdoor, I saw a couple of shadows running away from the side off my barn, hurry! get out here quick as possible, bye!" There he went to Pete's door and knocked just hard enough as not to wake the kid's. "Pete! Wake up, Pete! get out here quick, Pete! get up." Pete opened as fast as he could get at it. "What's the matter, the house not on fire is it?" Pete asked still on the sleepy side.

"Know that deep feeling I've been having lately?" He asked Pete, looking somewhat on the—stunned side. "I saw two shadows move across the side of the barn just a few minutes ago. Don't worry, I called the sheriff's; office, I guess it may take some time since we're so far out from town. We need to be on our guard for now, we mustn't wake up the kids, we don't want them to get scared." He sort of whispered to Pete. But, it wasn't that long that he said that, here comes the three boys to where they were. "What's the matter dad?" Chuck asked his father.

"I think we have trespassers on our property, I called and it might a while before they get here, so, watch it," Mr. Porter told the boys, taking great concern for all of them. They all took a window to see if they could spot the unwelcome guest lurking about. Sometime had passed, and then Iris came down to see what was going on.

"What you guys looking for this time of night?" She asked, sounded still half asleep and yawning.

"Uncle Bob saw a couple of peoples leaving around the barn out back," Johnathan told her, while keepings his eyes peering out the window curtain. Iris then folded her hands on her stomach starting to feel scared.

"It's pretty dark out there, keep a sharp eye out on anything that moves. We have to hold on till the law gets here." Mr. Porter told everyone. Iris got a spot next to Chuck and Tommy, she still kept her clutched hands tight against her stomach, Mr. porter told them he would go to the kitchen and see if anyone might come that way. Everyone kept watchful eye on the outside in front and the side window. Pete got that one, Johnathan meanwhile, kept a lookout at the front door, hoping to see whoever it was lurking about. It was silent for awhile until "Thump!" came to the side in which Pete was at, boy he moved backwards faster than they seen him move in a long time. Johnathan, suddenly, without thinking, opened the front door and stood a just stood inches from the doorway and hollered out loud, "OK! whoever you are . . . you better leave, and leave fast, we have the law coming and if you know what's good for ya', You! leave us be!" It was quiet, too quiet for them. So he went back in and shut the door and locked it fast. His Uncle came in the living room real quick, told his nephew that wasn't a good thing he did, that he could of got hurt and it wasn't worth the risk. Johnathan, looked' at the rest and knew his Uncle was right.

"I don't know what made me do that . . . maybe it because I care about you and all, I don't like these people trying to take what's yours and Chuck's, I Just care, that's all." Johnathan turned and looked at the door again, as though help would be there soon.

The storm died some more, then in a matter of time, three more loud thumps came to each sides of the place. Pete and Mr. Porter, raced to the windows to see anyone around the house. Still it was too dark and all they could see was nothing. Iris started to tremble and feel weakness in her legs. Tommy took notice and went over to let her know every thing was going to be fine.

"Uncle Bob, try calling the police again, tell them to hurry up . . . please!" Iris said near a loud voice.

So he did, this time he tried, there was nothing he heard except silence, cold dead silence. "Lines got to be down, or whoever's out there cut the wire." He told them as he hung it back up. Pete began rubbings his hair awhile so he could think of something to help out. But nothing came to mind, he was blank on ideas.

Then the heavy thumping started up again, the three of them this time came close to the side windows. Pete now was getting madder than a hornet, but being with the rest, he thought twice. Then, a loud voice was heard in the dark, "Robert! Do you hear me?" For a few seconds it got quiet, then the voice spoke once more, "We're here to get you and the others out of here, someone wants it, and he wants it now. How about it man? You leave off this land, no harm will come to you, hear?" Everyone inside just stared at each other, not saying a word, they were all kind of shocked that this was a happening. So, Mr. Porter walked over to the nearest of the windows, raised it just a couple of inches and he shouted out of it, "I don't want any trouble myself, but you and whoever's with you, will be arrested if you don't leave now! . . . I've done called the law, they should get here anytime now, so just leave us alone!" He then closed it back down and hoped for the best. "Well, I've gave them my warning . . . hope nothing happens till we can get the Sheriff and Deputies out here." He told everyone, as they just looked at him for that bit of assurance. Then the pounding started, again, this time they seemed to be getting closer to the house as the pounding got louder each time they would throw 'em another round.

Chuck and Johnathan got to looking out one of the side windows, and to their surprise, three shadowy figures come into view. Chuck got to take a long hard stare at them, then he called his—dad over for a look. "Do those guys look familiar too you at all?" Chuck asked his father, as he got his cousin to move and let his dad get a look.

"They do look kind of familiar, bur I just can't place 'em right off." Mr. Porter told his son, trying to think deeply of who these guys were. Then, another voice hollered out of the night, "All right! you heard what I want Mr. Porter, do you want to get off peaceful . . . or, go about this the hard way, which do you prefer now?"

Then it dawned on him who that voice came from, his one time friend years ago, Carl Lucas. They use to do business together on different projects, till Carl got greedy, and wanted more than his share of money. "Carl! I don't want any kind of trouble with you!" Mr. Porter shouted out loud enough for them to hear. "Why do you want my place, don't you already have enough of your own?" He asked him with a concerned voice, maybe to let Carl think it over. He went to the front door, waited a few second's, and took the doorknob in his right hand, and turned it slowly to open the door. Then he took a few steps out from under the doorway. Looking into the darkness, there stood four figures instead of three. He strained his eyes to focus on the other three standing next to him. As he looked and strained his eyes, then, he recognized who they were, Dale, Philip and Larry, the Hanley Brothers. No one ever got close enough to ever know that they were low down and always up to meanness. Whatever they could do to make a few dollars, they would do it. Then Carl Lucas spoke once again, to get his message loud and clear.

"Robert! I'm telling you now, leave now, I don't, I don't nobody to get hurt, please give up this worthless piece of land, it's for the best for all of us," Then, without really thinking what he was doing, Mr. Porter decided it was time to get this matter over and done, he was on the brink of fighting now. When he got close to all four men, he began to speak with a clear tone, "I don't care one little bit about your threats on me . . . but since I have family in there, you've said as much as I can put up with, I want you and these three off this place as fast as you can, if not, when the law . . .

"Bob, Bob, Bob," Mr. Lucas repeated at Mr. Porter, as he started taking a step at time, being in no mood now, to a battle-of-words, Mr. Porter began to take a step back, as Mr. Lucas stepped forward toward him. Everyone inside, watched in hopes, that soon, a fight was about to happen. The Hanley brothers followed each step that Mr. Lucas took, it didn't look too good at all, not one bit at all. Chuck and the others, grabbed their coats and something to fight with if that was what it was coming down to. They all rushed out the door, Pete coming out last, Chuck and Johnathan on each side of Mr. Porter, Pete and Iris, behind them.

Carl Lucas and the Hanley brothers, they seemed amused, it just made it even better to have them all together, when it was over with, to have them on the ground, side by side.

A flash of lightning made it somewhat easier to get a glance at who'd they maybe up against. Chuck had in his left hand, his trusty ball bat, Pete and Johnathan, both had pokers slightly raised. As for Iris, she had her long nails.

"Please Bob, think of these kids, don't have them getting hurt because your too stubborn to let go of land, that's worthless!" Mr. Lucas shouted out to all of them in sight.

"Can't do it. My Great Grandfather and my Father, worked [[cannot read]] it!" Mr. Porter fired back at him, Mr. Lucas just stared at him with a slight grin on his small rounded face. Well, one could see, he wasn't giving up, not one bit at all, "OK boys, lets, lets do this quickly, I got other things to do, so get busy," As they slowly came at them, they heard something off in the distance. It was the sound of a bugle sound of "Charge", everyone was stunned, Mr. Porter and his bunch, turned behind them, and saw what looked liked, horsemen, charging down the hill and coming in their direction. Their eyes as far as they could see, had a yellowish glow, even the horses eyes looked the same. The Hanley boys and Mr. Lucas, just, stood, with horror on their faces. As they came closer at them, all body function quit working, so scared to move, they just shook with fear. As Mr. Porter and the others moved to safety as the horsemen were soon upon them. When Mr. Lucas and his boys had gotten the strength to make their move and get away, it was too late. They were trapped from running in any direction. The horsemen had them in a circle, starring with 'em with their dead glowing eyes, waiting to go into action.

"L-Look, we don't have a beef w-with you guys, just let us leave, we'll just call this off and nobody gets hurt, so hows 'bout it, deal?" Mr. Lucas asked while holding his own.

The head horsemen just looked at him, not speaking a word. He made a slow turn of his head to Mr. Porter, who was standing on the porch with the rest of his family. Looking at him for a moment and smiled. Then, he spoke.

"You have made me proud. You all were ready to fight for what belongs to us all. This land will stay ours, for generations that will follow you, I'm very proud of you, a fine gentleman you are." Turning his head back to the ones in front on the ground, he spoke to them, "As for you, I shall run you to the ends of the earth, till you can run no more!" Then he let out a loud cry of command as he drew his sword to the air, "Forward . . . hoooo." Then, they began the chase, swooshing all about Carl and his so called boys. They thought they were on fire as the horses shot hot air from their nostrils and rising on their hinds as to come down upon them, Carl and the Hanley boys tried running to their truck, but it didn't work out that way, the horsemen cut 'em off before they could get to it.

Pete was in amazement at this whole ordeal, in fact, he in his own way, felt sorry for them. But for Pete, it was better them, than him. Iris was bewildered by watching these bad men running for their dear lives. Her sharp fingernails dug into Johnathan's shoulders as she felt great horror of seeing this great apparition before her very own eyes, Johnathan was so spellbound at this weird attraction, that he couldn't feel what she was doing to him. There was so much screaming and the hollering, that one could imagine what one would suffer in hell. The horsemen never let up on those poor devils, but they were getting their just deserts. It wasn't long till Carl Lucas and his henchmen, were out of sight in the darkness. But their screams, faded with them. Everyone stood in cold silence, it seemed that their problems was over with. Pete looked at Mr. Porter with a very confused look of shock. The kids held on to one another, as though something still had a hold on them.

It wasn't too long that the sheriff and two of his deputies showed up. Sheriff Webber got out and walked to the front porch where they were standing, still in disbelief.

"We got here as best as we could. The roads were slowing us down being in the muddy shape they were in. What in the world is going on out here Bob?" Sheriff Webber, asked, wiping the rain from the right side of his face.

They all looked down at him at the same time, then with a low solemn tone, Mr. Porter spoke. "You wouldn't believe me or the rest at what we just seen, you just wouldn't." "Tell me Pete, what went on out here!"

"Sheriff . . ." Pete started saying, as his eyes looked back out to the darkness where he last saw Carl and the rest were last seen running. "I saw it, and I still can't believe it myself, not one bit." Sheriff Webber could tell, that something had to of happen to make these folks act the way they did. Looking toward the ground and his men, he looked back at them and asked, "Pete, got any coffee made up we can have?" Pete finally to snap out of it, he replied back quickly, "yeah, sure, got a fresh pot I made before this all came along. Come in, I think I'll have me some myself." Everyone headed into the house and to the table in the kitchen. Pete poured them all coffee and began to go over the whole story, with Mr. Porter in the lead. After two hours of going over the event, the Sheriff thought they would check around the place and go around the roadway, maybe they would run into them somewhere in the area. Then they headed out to see if they could find some trace that he might be able to catch up with them. After they drove off searching in the night for Carl and his boys, Chuck got somewhat tired when he saw how late it had gotten. Everyone agreed also, they were all drained from all that went on. As they headed for the stairs, Iris turned back to look at the picture in the dinning room on the wall. As she stared at it, it was as though Major Porter was smiling back at her, then she got a cold shiver up heir spine, then, she followed the rest, but real fast.

It them a while, finally, they were getting a goodnights sleep. Nobody bothered to stay awake, not even good 'ol Pete. He was snoring up a blue stormy one might say.

It was after eight thirty when Pete had woken from a restful nights sleep. After he had gotten dressed, knowing it was time to get breakfast going. He glanced a moment out the kitchen window, it turned out to be a beautiful morning. Iris came down and went to the kitchen for a glass of milk. She saw Pete just getting the coffee made, she then went over to him and out of the blue, gave him a big hug, He was kind of surprised at this, but, it was a good feeling he never got in a long time.

"Oh Pete, it's such a pretty morning, after having all that rain. If you don't mind, I'll help you fix breakfast, ok?" She asked with a bright smile that nobody at all could turn down, "Sure you can! Get the eggs, bacon and the cheese out, I'll get the pan heated up." So she got everything from the refrigerator, and sat them together. It wasn't too long that the rest got up after smelling all the good aroma that worked it's way up to them. Pete was almost through with the bacon and Iris had a few pieces of toast to go along with the rest of what was fixed. Mr. Porter made his way into the kitchen, then the two boys, Chuck was in lead as usual. Last night was still fresh in their minds as they tried to have a good breakfast. Pete sat his fork down, on the table and looked over at Mr. Porter and asked in a concerned voice.

"Do you reckon that they might of found those scoundrels by now Bob?" Chuck's father put down his coffee cup and he wiped around his mouth and sat his hands down in front of him and replied, "I was wondering myself Pete, maybe I ought to give the Sheriff a call, they may have caught up with them somewhere down the road, I hate how scared those poor fools were, but, they got what they asked for and more."

After he had enough to eat, Mr. Porter got in touch with Sheriff Webber. He told him they searched and searched, but they were nowhere to be seen. So Mr. Porter thanked him and hung up. He got everyone together and told them what he was told by the Sheriff, in some way now, they felt a bit sorry for them guys, but what was done, was done.

Chapter Twenty

The kids decided that since it was a nice day to get out, to check around the place and see how things where. Each of them shoving the other out of the way, just getting to the front door, Mr. Porter and Pete meanwhile, that they ought to get things back into swing when all of a sudden, they heard Chuck and the others holler for him to come quick. He ran as fast as he could to where they were at. He looked toward the ground and saw Clairabel lying down on her side.

The kids were afraid she was sick or something, to them she was in a lot of pain, "Iris, go tell Pete that I'll need some old sheets and a blanket, we're about to have a new addition to the family, hurry!" He told her, as he got to his knees and began rubbing the left side of her neck.

"There, there now, now girl, we're going to take real, I mean, real good care of you, you know, don't you girl?" He was telling her in a soothing voice. Then he turned to Chuck and Johnathan, he told them to fetch up some good hot water, and not to loose any of it if possible, he'll need all he can use. Off they went as fast as their feet and legs could take them to get hot water for the cow who at anytime was about to give birth. They past Iris, as she was heading on back to where Chuck's dad was waiting for them.

"Here Uncle Bob, Pete said he'll be down to help as soon as he can." She handed him the old sheets first, then, the blankets. Iris looked at Clairabel with a lot of compassion for her, that everything would be ok.

The other three finally showed up at the scene, each had a pale of hot water a piece in their hands, Pete as soon as he sat his pale on the ground, he rolled his sleeves up to help Mr. Porter when it came the time. Clairabel began to loud mooing sounds, she began to slightly shift side to side till she came to another of her rest time. "Alright Pete, if this goes well, hold down on her back and I'll get the head of the calf when it appears, ok, be ready now!" He told Pete as Clairabel began: acting up again. Chuck and the others, I must say, was watching this thing as though the Devil himself was about to be horned himself. Their hearts a beating as one could imagine, just the way it was when those horsemen showed up like they did last night. But! For these kids, they where about to witness life coming into the world for the first time in their life. Time was drawing near, they had to be ready at the sign of the calf showing it's head, they had to act quickly, A few more minutes flow by, Clairabel was a showing some signs that she was ready for the big event of giving birth. Then, all of a sudden, it all started to happen. She began to what looked like a pushing motion, then two more as she began mooing louder, Iris began biting her fingernails in suspense, Chuck, he had his mouth so wide opened that a bus could right go into it, Johnathan on the other hand, was biting on his lower lip in hopes that everything would just go alright. The moment finally come, the head began a popping through, his Uncle waited till it was really out enough to get a good hold to help pull the whole calf all the way out. Pete was holding the back side just hard enough to let Mr. Porter get a good grip to pull the calf all the way out. Suddenly, it was over. It didn't seem too long of time that this miracle took place. Chucks Father took the blanket to wrap the calf in, he asked Iris if she would like a chance to finish cleaning it up. She got down on her knees and began wiping it off. A huge smile appeared on her face, as she gently moved the blanket over it.

"Boy! That was the fastest come in this world thing I have ever seen. What do you guys think of him?"

"He sure is cute, but looks kind of small." Chuck replied back while scratching the back of his head.

Johnathan and Pete stood side by side each other while Iris was still cleaning up the newborn calf, they had big grins across their faces watching her. Looking about the land around them, Mr. Porter looked back smiling at them and said, "Well, since Pete and I helped get this new calf here, somebody needs to give him a good name, don't you think so Pete?" he asked him.

"Why, yes, sure he's got to have an up and good one, yep, a good one." The kids to think what would be a good name to call the baby calf, there it came, "Since he came into this world a charging just like the spirit of those Calvary men, how's about that we call him, "Calvary." All the guys kicked about and it sounded good, real good. Chuck and Johnathan bent down and did a small christening ceremony and then with a loud voice they spoke his name, "Hail Calvary, may you run this pasture forever!" Clairabel let out a mooing that she approved of it also, everyone began to laugh at her, Calvary was going to fit in well, real well.

The End